# THE HAWK AND THE SUN

*Abram dwelled in the land of Canaan,
and Lot dwelled in the cities of the plain,
and pitched his tent toward Sodom.*

— GENESIS 13.12

# THE HAWK
# AND THE SUN

## A Novel by Byron Herbert Reece

*Foreword by Hugh Ruppersburg*

*Brown Thrasher Books*

THE UNIVERSITY OF GEORGIA PRESS

*Athens and London*

Published in 1994 as a Brown Thrasher Book
by the University of Georgia Press
Athens, Georgia 30602
© 1955 by E. P. Dutton & Co., Inc.
© 1983 by Eva Mae Reece
Foreword to the Brown Thrasher edition
© 1994 by the University of Georgia Press
Reprinted by permission of Kate Reece Lane
All rights reserved

The paper in this book meets the guidelines
for permanence and durability of the Committee on
Production Guidelines for Book Longevity
of the Council on Library Resources.

Printed in the United States of America
98  97  96  95  94  P  5  4  3  2  1

Library of Congress Cataloging in Publication Data

Reece, Byron Herbert, 1917–1958.
The hawk and the sun / Byron Herbert Reece ; foreword by
Hugh Ruppersburg.
p.    cm.
"Brown Thrasher books."
ISBN 0-8203-1656-3 (pbk. alk. paper)
1. City and town life—Southern States—Fiction.  2. Southern
States—Race relations—Fiction.  3. Young men—Southern States—
Fiction.  4. Racism—Southern States—Fiction.  5. Lynching—
Fiction.  I. Title.
PS3535.E245H38  1994          94-15267
813'.54—dc20

British Library Cataloging in Publication Data available

*The Hawk and the Sun* was originally published in 1955
by E. P. Dutton & Co., Inc., New York.

*For*

EVA MAE REECE

# Contents

# Foreword

## Hugh Ruppersburg

Byron Herbert Reece's first novel, *Better a Dinner of Herbs*, was published by E. P. Dutton in 1950 to generally favorable reviews. Reece had labored on the novel since 1945, often at night, for during the day he had worked the fields of his parents' farm near Blood Mountain in North Georgia. In 1945 he had published a volume of poems, *Ballad of the Bones*. A second collection of verse, *Bow Down in Jericho*, appeared shortly after the novel in 1950. Two other volumes followed in the next few years.

Reece began work on his second novel shortly after the publication of his first, but he made slow progress. In her biographical essay on Reece, *The Bitter Berry: The Life of Byron Herbert Reece*, Bettie Sellers chronicles the difficulties he experienced in the five years he worked on the book. He spent the summer of 1950 teaching literature at the University of California in Los Angeles but was barely able to earn living expenses. His father's worsening illness in 1951 demanded more of his time on the family farm, and he taught for a while at Young Harris College to pay expenses. A Guggenheim fellowship in 1952 did allow him to turn more of his attention to the novel. Always in bad health, he was diagnosed early in 1954 with tuberculosis, the same disease that was to kill both his parents. After several months in a sanatorium, he emerged to resume work on the book, though his mother's death in the summer of 1954 only worsened matters.

*The Hawk and the Sun* finally appeared in 1955 to mixed reviews. Its focus on a lynching, and a strong element of sex and homoeroticism, made some reviewers uncomfortable. The *New Yorker* dismissed the book for its presentation of what "can hardly be called a complete story. The meaningless lynching, which changes nothing, differs from other meaningless acts only in the depth of its brutality." The *Saturday Review*, though praising the book, called it "appalling" and emphasized the roles of the lynching and sex. The *New York Herald* commended the novel for its "luminous clarity" and for how it brought, "by the sheer excellence of the writing, a new freshness and force" to scenes and subjects that had been often described by earlier writers. Local reviews were generally positive. Still, the book did little to change the public perception of Reece as a poet—a perception that was in fact accurate but that focused attention away from the novels. Several writers for the Atlanta newspapers, most notably Ralph McGill, repeatedly called attention to Reece's work, and Reece began to see his reputation as a poet grow both locally and nationally. In 1958 he had signed a contract for the first volume of a trilogy of novels about the history of North Georgia, but his physical and emotional health continued to worsen, and he committed suicide in the fall of 1958 at Young Harris College.

Reece was much mourned by those few who knew him, but the modest reputation his poetry and novels had earned him soon faded. Today he is virtually unknown outside his home state, and even there his name rings with only vague familiarity in those ears that recognize it.

This is a pity. Reece was a poet of freshness and originality who favored the dignified simplicity of the English folk ballad and the King James Bible over the flamboyant and less accessible style of twentieth-century modernism. The fact that Reece was absolutely out of step with contemporary trends in modern poetry would have dissuaded many from taking seriously the deceptively simple cadences of his verse. Just as unfortunate as his obscure reputation as a poet is the absolute neglect of his two fine novels, *Better a Dinner of Herbs* and *The Hawk and the Sun*—works much more reflective than his poetry of developments in modern writing. One is always aware in these novels that the writer is a poet. Each sentence is finely crafted. Descriptions are expertly drawn, with a moving lyricism that in only a few words evokes vivid visual images. Each paragraph, each chapter, moves with a clear and subtle rhythm, and the novels themselves are structured in a way uniquely suited to the stories they tell.

Reece's second novel, *The Hawk and the Sun*, is a narrative morality play about a day in the life of a small southern town. In this sense it reminds us of such literary encomia to small-town American life as Thornton Wilder's *Our Town* or Sherwood Anderson's *Winesburg, Ohio*. Each chapter moves from one townsperson to another. The town librarian, an aging matron, a deranged widow, an old farmer, a wandering hunter, a crippled black man, and three children in early adolescence are the citizens whose perspectives tell the town's tale. Without the sentimentality of Wilder, or the underlying psychological torment in Anderson, Reece works at his town of Tilden with a different method. Wilder's play follows over the course of many years the lives and deaths of his characters as they grow up, marry, and raise families. Anderson traces the growth of a young man, George Willard, who proves he has achieved maturity in the last chapter by leaving his town forever. Reece, who certainly knew these two works and was well read in modern American fiction in general, focuses on a single day in the town of Tilden. It is a typical day on the one hand, and atypical on the other, for it is the day on which the only black man in town, a crippled handyman named Dandelion, is lynched for his alleged rape of the deranged widow.

Here lies the second dimension of the novel, a severe examination of racism, small-town provincialism, and murder in mid-twentieth-century America. In this sense Reece writes in the same vein as such predecessors as Theodore Dreiser, William Faulkner, Jean Toomer, Thomas Wolfe, Erskine Caldwell, and Lillian Smith, and of these only Faulkner surpasses Reece in his depiction and understanding of the social, moral, and cultural forces that lead to the horrific communal ritual of a lynching.

Just as he makes Tilden the archetypal American small town with its varied cast of characters, so does Reece present a lynching whose details are so familiar that it seems almost stereotypical. Reacting to a rumor of rape whose truth they never bother to check, a crowd of largely ignorant townsmen decide to avenge the crime by lynching the accused man. That Dandelion is black seems automatically to convict him in their minds, and they easily overlook his advanced age and his misshapen legs. As the sun inexorably wends its way through the sky, the crowd gathers and makes its plans, and word gradually spreads of what is afoot. A "dark boy" named Farley, bothered and concerned, runs to tell his father, who is the town librarian and a history teacher at the local high school. Reece makes clear that the librarian is Dandelion's only hope, but poor hope he proves to be. He seeks help from the local sheriff, who feigns concern and claims helplessness, and who later sends word to the mob to hurry up with its plans so that the librarian will not be able to save the man. The librarian pleads for help from the town minister, who claims to be powerless to stop the mob, but who offers to pray for Dandelion's soul. The black man's death, he intones, is part of a pattern beyond his control: "At the foundation of the world Tilden was scheming against the life of the Negro Dandelion. And Tilden will take the life of Dandelion because the world advanced as it advanced and not as it might have." The town banker refuses to help, explaining that it is his "policy never to meddle in the private affairs of [his] depositors." In a perhaps deliberately clumsy way Reece shows how the librarian muses over the similarities between the town's preparations for what is about to happen and events from past history, such as the Battle of Waterloo. History is the librarian's solace. It tells him that events occur inevitably, that they are beyond the control of mortal human hands, so that the librarian delays until, by the time he finally arrives at Dandelion's house to help him escape, the mob has already captured him and dragged him off to the woods. History for the librarian justifies his moral cowardice. In the end, all he can do is stumble into the woods long after Dandelion is dead to bury him.

The sheriff, the librarian, the banker, and the preacher, men of justice, intellect, commerce, and God, are too weak to stop the lynching. Disapprove though they may, they cannot bring themselves to face down the mob. By their own passivity and rationalizing, by their unwillingness to contravene the deep codes of the community that they know to be wrong, they are as responsible for the murder as if they had committed it themselves.

Like other writers before him, Reece takes pains to make clear that the lynching of Dandelion is an act in which virtually every member of the community participates, either by active involvement or by indifference or by silence. In his novel *Light in August*, William Faulkner dramatized a town's knowledge of, and acquiescence to, a lynching by focusing on the perspectives of various townspeople who talk about the murder the victim of the lynching supposedly committed. After the lynching, Faulkner describes how they sit at dinner, discussing the killing, already a part of the town's history. In a story he called "The Child by Tiger," Thomas Wolfe describes how townspeople stand in awe before an undertaker's window in which a black man's corpse, riddled with bullets, hangs as proof of the vigilante justice that has been rendered. Lillian Smith, in her novel *Strange Fruit*, devotes a long Joycean chapter to brief episodic glimpses of activities and people on the evening a lynching has occurred.

Reece takes a similar approach, yet he confines the entire novel to a single day. Early on he makes clear that the day will end in Dandelion's murder, and the result is a sense of inevitability that gives the narrative the fatal quality of a folk ballad about death and love lost. By this stratagem, Reece relieves the reader's suspense about the impending murder and concentrates instead on how that murder came to be. His approach is doggedly objective and impersonal, almost as if he is writing a factual history, a documentary detective story. He allows the reader little easy sympathy for any character—if we come to feel close to any of them—to the librarian for instance, or to his son—we do so almost in spite of the novelist's efforts. Reece keeps the reader at arm's distance by referring to characters repeatedly with labels or phrases that deprive them of their individualistic humanity and instead insist on their roles in the gruesome ritual the community is acting out. Farley is thus the "dark boy" or "the boy Farley," while his friend Jonathan is the "blond boy"; Farley's father is the "librarian" or "the father of the boy Farley"; the minister of the First Church of Tilden is "the Reverend Mr. Carhorn" (an appellation repeated with vicious, biting irony). Dandelion is "the Negro Dandelion." We are never allowed to forget the roles these characters play as the novel's tragic drama unfolds.

This novel's subject is not so much the murderous consequences of racism as it is the debilitating effects of blind adherence to destructive social codes and rituals. The impersonal way in which characters are presented suggests that they are pawns in a game over which they have no control. In this sense the novel seems decidedly naturalistic, though it does not quite endorse the notion that Dandelion's murder is truly inevitable. Sufficient attention is paid to the sheriff's indifference, the minister's feigned helplessness, and the librarian's weak musings over the inevitability of history to suggest that the murder could have been prevented had someone shown the courage.

In many ways *The Hawk and the Sun* betrays the image of Byron Herbert Reece that faintly persists in his native region, that of a mountain poet whose rustic ballads commemorate with stoic simplicity the virtues of country life. The severity with which his second novel examines his native region suggests quite a different sort of writer than that image implies. Another element that reveals a more complex writer than has been imagined is the homoeroticism in both his novels. Both *Better a Dinner of Herbs* and *The Hawk and the Sun* portray adolescent boys who have brief homosexual relationships with other boys. Reece seems to portray such relationships as part of the normal process of sexual exploration and awakening, though he counterpoints them with other heterosexual relationships. In *The Hawk and the Sun*, Farley, who is attracted to the blond boy Jonathan, is also attracted to the girl Rhoda, with whom he had a sexual encounter the day before the one on which the novel focuses. In the present time of the novel Farley pursues Jonathan throughout the course of the day's events, until finally they have sex after watching the murder of Dandelion. (This linkage of homoerotic sex and death is foreshadowed earlier in the book when Rhoda strangles a cat as she watches the two boys wrestle on the ground.)

The knowledge that murder and death impart is one form of initiation into the adult world of sin and experience (the world into which the boys who witness the lynching in Allen Tate's poem "The Swimmers" are initiated). Sexual experience, homosexual or heterosexual, enacts a similar entry into adulthood. It is not clear to me, just yet, exactly how Reece means these homosexual episodes to be seen. It is too easy to write them off as examples of the world's corruption, of the Sodom alluded to in the novel's epigraph and with which in some way the town of Tilden is equated. In a letter cited by Bettie Sellers in her biography of Reece, the poet makes clear that he does not necessarily regard homosexual love as perversion. His poems about the biblical friendship of David and Jonathan, for instance, treat homosexual love in an appreciative, positive manner. What is clear is that sex and death in both novels are powerfully interrelated—closely linked yet diametrically opposed elements of the life force that animates the world he envisions.

Frequently in the novel Reece refers to the sun's position in the sky as a way of making clear the time of day and of stressing the apparent inevitability with which events move toward the murder that will occur before the sun goes down. The sun shares with the hawk a place in the novel's title, whose meaning comes clear in the closing sentences of the final chapter. An elderly farmer named Abraham sits that night with his kinfolk at supper, perhaps thinking of the murder he tried briefly that day to prevent, and of his retreat before the hostility of the mob that threatened him:

> He looked at Sarah's pale, patient face and wanted to say something more, but nothing came. He could not shape the words. In the silence that followed his speech the family fell to eating with heartiness. He looked at their faces and he knew then that beyond the death of them all the hawk would lift. Except the sun the hawk, Abraham thought as he poised his fork above his plate, and forever the hawk; the hawk and the sun. (192)

The sun signifies time, human mortality, the transience of all things. The hawk is the judging mind of God, who

xvii

will when the sun sets render salvation or damnation to all human souls. Reece suggests in this final symbol that those who killed Dandelion, or who did not act to stop his death, will be judged, and that although human justice failed Dandelion in the town of Tilden, divine justice will not fail him. Punishment will be meted out to those who have transgressed. This is the only justice, however fleeting and implied, that Reece allows in his novel.

Like *Better a Dinner of Herbs*, *The Hawk and the Sun* is replete with vivid, beautiful images of life's mystery. It is a somber, guarded work, much darker than the first novel. It makes no excuses for the murder it describes. It does not ask for understanding of the mob that carries out the crime, and it certainly shows no mercy of its own. It is unrelenting and unsparing in the condemnation it expresses for the horror it portrays. Thus it is easy to overlook this book, to turn back to the poetry, or to the first novel, or to the carefully staged photographs of Reece at work in his fields or in his study, those images of an unthreatening and simple man, not the stern and severe moralist who understood his region and his kind more deeply than we could ever suspect or want.

# Part I

# MORNING

# I

It was three o'clock, and as the tide of darkness rose again over Tilden and flowed westward after the ebbing moon a man stood in his open doorway and looked out upon the dark street. The houses on the opposite side of the street, and up and down it, were barely visible shapes formed of denser darkness than the darkness of the night. The maple boughs moved in a light wind and he heard their faint sound but he could not see them. Now he did not try to visualize them any more than he tried to visualize the hid motions of his heart which he had thought of once in the image of a hand fisted and then flexed until his arm was tired. That was long ago. Something had happened to the sinews of his imagination, or he had only grown up. He no longer visualized the action of his heart, nor the movement of the maple boughs. The movements were too familiar.

Or too strange, he thought to himself, though he had planted the maples when they were seedlings along the frontage of his own lot and remembered the whole file of them along the street, from leapfrog height. Now and then as he stared into the street a cargo of light without carrier moved along it. It was a dim light, revealing nothing distinctly except once the sidewalk opposite him. A beam revealed a break in the concrete of the sidewalk where two sections abutted, an irregular quarter-circle joining two sides of a right angle, like a corner torn roughly from a square of paper, the broken part sunk a little below the rest. But then it was dark again and he could not see it. Perhaps it was in his mind and lighted by memory, the sun of fragments and wholes that shone more than the now moon, low, its light sheared intermittently by clouds, sinking behind him and sending its carriageless cargoes of light across the town.

Behind the man was the bed he had quitted momentarily with promise of resumption of his broken sleep. He would turn again into his house after a breath of air. As he stood, not turning yet, he felt the life of the town surrounding him but shapeless in sleep and darkness and lacking even the density of substance that formed the houses against the lesser darkness of the night. His mind could not enter the shut doors and stare to shape the sleepers of Tilden. He was aware only that the people slept, making their shapes beneath covers; some alone and others two by two yet divided by the insuperable fact of their separateness.

When he turned into his house again the town dimly lighted by the sinking moon and the life of it which had been lifted from the deep of nothing to an amorphous shape in his mind, secret now, dropped uncreated into darkness and undivided sleep hollowed by cells of dreams.

Somewhere in the town one dreamed of Thebes. One dreamed of a tin of snuff, another of the cat Tawm's arch and spit of pride; and one, sleeping or waking, dreamed of the flesh and bones of the blond boy Jonathan as he, integer, moved separate but indivisible from the life of the town which the sun created anew each day into the definition of light.

# II

IN THAT utter darkness of just before dawn the Negro Dandelion woke in his rotted house on the outskirts of Tilden to the jangling sound of a clock alarm. He hushed the clatter of the cheap alarm clock that rested on an upended crate by his bed, reaching a black, sinewy, bare arm out from the greasy covers and pushing down on the stem. He rose to a sitting position and lit a kerosene lamp that stood on the crate by the noisy clock. When there was light in the room he turned his head slowly and searched out all the corners. When he saw that nothing was changed, that nothing was out of place or pushed away from the wall to make a hiding place, he eased his body from the bed and fumbled on his clothes.

For a moment the Negro Dandelion stood yawning and wiping his mouth as if to remove from his lips the taste of sleep. Then he searched his pocket for the snuff tin, and it was there, but he remembered before taking it from his pocket even that it was empty.

He made a sound, nasal but patient. Naah, he said. He took the tin from his pocket and opened it and looked into it, but of course it was empty. He had emptied it the night before. Carefully he put the lid back on the tin and returned it to the bib pocket of his overalls.

15

That's what I dreamt about, he said. His voice was patient.

He drooped his lower lip as if it were full of snuff and stepped through the door of his shack into the darkness outside. The sun was not up yet. He stood a moment in the dim light but the lack of snuff made the morning tasteless and he began to move down the dirt path that led from his house to the street.

Dandelion moved obsequiously through the town of Tilden, shuffling in grotesque good humor from odd job to odd job. He was lame. His legs were withered to the misshapen bones of shin and thigh. It was said that his lameness resulted from the pleasure his mother took in men. It was told that the disease she had contracted in the pursuit of her pleasure not only deformed the child Dandelion and reddened the eyes of the young buck Negroes that once lived on the outer fringe of Tilden, but withered the pride of many white men as well. The white women of Tilden were glad when Hattie, the mother of Dandelion, became demonstrably affected: if their husbands remained free of any taint of her disease they were exonerated of association with Hattie.

Dandelion never reflected on the cause of his lameness, but if he had it is probable he would not have begrudged his mother her parlous pleasure. It was the only pleasure she had except one. She loved to dip snuff. After she grew old and obviously riddled by the disease, from fear of contamination the matrons of the town withheld their washing from her. When she was outcast altogether she lived on the nickels and dimes her deformed offspring managed to collect for emptying garbage cans and cleaning outhouses and chicken sheds. Now and then he spared a dime for a box of snuff for Hattie, and then she sat in her chair, stiff from creeping paresis, and spat happily into the brown dirt of her bare yard. She was sitting thus when she felt a force strike suddenly within her like interior lightning and fell forward out of her chair and lay dead on the floor.

After Hattie died Dandelion lived alone and continued in his odd-job orbit about the town of Tilden. He had grown middle-aged in it and now he was held in affectionate tolerance by most of the town's families. But the sound of his footsteps as he shuffled along in his lameness was hesitant, like the sound of an October leaf scraping against a wall.

His lame shuffle now served to advance him, a scarecrow tatter of a man, down to the street and toward the heart of the town yet indistinct in the gray light of dawn. He measured in his mind the length of the circuit of his customary chores, for he could not go to the store and buy a tin of snuff before he had completed his rounds. It was a fire to build, it was a house to sweep, it was water to draw to a dip of snuff. He had also to collect some change from one or another of his patrons in order to afford the snuff. His big flat index finger probing the recesses of his pockets encountered nothing rounded in the fine indubitable circle-shapes of coins.

I must have dreamt it, he said, making himself patient about the snuff. No matter the length of the circuit he would have completed it before the stores opened their doors for business.

It was a shed to clean, it was a chicken to dress, it was wood to cart; without snuff it was a long time till eight o'clock.

# III

A SINGLE hunter with his hounds in the hills near the place
of the farmer Abraham was awake and aware when the
weight of darkness balanced on the slow pivot of midnight
and began to dip toward dawn. The fox was in his lair and
would not be roused, and the hounds smelled out the runs
in the hills and only questioned now and then the faint odor
of a cold track with loud, melancholy, indecisive voices.

The name of the hunter was Nimrod Anse, and no one,
not even he, knew where he had got his name. He sat with
his back against a tree on the point of the highest hill and
listened to the questioning voices of the hounds. Below him
Tilden lay in total darkness in a bowl of earth and slept the
drenched sleep of mid-August night. Toward four o'clock
the moon that had lighted the town vaguely for the watcher
in his doorway dropped as if by sudden ordination behind
the hill on which Nimrod Anse sat and the darkness seamed
itself against all light until the sun should rise.

To the eye of the hunter, as to that disembodied eye in
which all things have their being, after the sun began to rise
the oblong of darkness in which Tilden was still submerged
looked like a black atoll jutting above seas of running light.
As the sun rose higher the morning mists shifting and coiling
among the low rounded hills rolled the rays from one to another in a strict illusion of flow. When Tilden itself began
to be visible the dark island seemed cast upon by the debris

of flood. The first wash of light that swept it from two sides strewed it with the tops of trees and suddenly as the whole town was inundated the spired First Church of Tilden sprang afloat as if chosen ark in a latter Flood. Hunter Anse watched it as it wallowed, or seemed to wallow, ponderously afloat among the housetops and the roofs of shops and stores riding level or listing askew in the illuminating flood.

To the eye of the hunter on the higher ground that surrounded Tilden the situation of the town was discovered sharp and clear by the risen sun. Behind Tilden mountains low and rounded rose on three sides. Not close but like a distant irregular semicircular wall thrown up against invasion from the world outside. To the east the country opened into flat plains that stretched to the sea. In this direction there was no obstacle or impediment against invasion. It was as if the trust of Tilden bred to the sea itself to moat it on its one vulnerable side. There was, of course, no need to guard against invasion of any sort, for the old town had reached the point of balance where its population remained constant, being only momentarily unbalanced in the one direction or the other by a birth or a death. There was little in the town to lure outsiders into it, but for all that the inhabitants could think of no very good reasons for leaving it. It was a comfortable town, except for minority peoples, and all these who at one time or another had tried their luck in the town had gone elsewhere with the exception of the lame Negro Dandelion.

Now and again a young man or woman of Tilden knew such ambition it drove them out to seek wider horizons, and these left the town by way of the north. Contrary to appearances it was to the north that the arterial highway led, threading into the hills until it found a gap toward which it lifted for the last few miles of ascent along the face of a ridge like a heavy line marking a graph of flight.

Hunter Nimrod Anse, from his position in the hills to the west, followed this line with his eyes until he became aware that his treasonable mind fled along it from his only possible home. He dropped his eyes again to Tilden. It was near seven o'clock and the town, houses and streets which had been shut to the night watcher, lay open now in August sunlight like a long-kept secret declared.

# IV

It was a quarter of a mile from Dandelion's to the first house with a white occupant. At mid-distance he could see, when it was light, his own house and the house where the white woman lived. Here he was at the point of a shallow arc the street made in curving gently around the toe bulge of a low ridge.

Once he passed this point and lost sight of his own house he felt himself in enemy territory and his skin prickled. He knew without once looking up to see them how as soon as he was in sight of the white woman's house two eyes stared out at him. They were secret and hostile, darting out at him through the dirty little window whose glass was discolored like a surface of water stained by a drop of oil. Like quick birds the two eyes darted out through the morning light for their view of him and then to secret again, as if afraid he would glance up suddenly and find them watching him.

He passed within a few feet of the house and below it. The box-square house was built against an elevation that rose several feet above the street level. The front was four or five feet from the ground and was supported by square brick pillars while the rear of the house rested against the earth. He could look up and see the sills and the sleepers that supported the flooring. Among the litter of accumulated cast-offs and boxes and broken chairs the plumbing was visible like a network of exposed bowels. The Negro kept his eyes averted from the house as he passed out of a sense of innate decency, turning his gaze from it as he would from a wind-lifted skirt. For the distance he was in sight of the house he always hurried as much as possible, humping forward in his grotesque shuffling walk.

When he had passed, the secret, hostile eyes of the white woman followed him as they had watched him since he had first come into sight.

That nigger, the woman said.

Her hands stilled in the dirty water of the stained sink as she leaned into the window as far as she could to watch him up the street. She brushed furiously at the glass where it was stained and flawed, obscuring the figure, elongating and con-torting it like a trick mirror, as the Negro passed from view. She had realized time and again that the flaw in the window-pane was there from the cast, yet each morning she tried to wipe the glass clear so that for a moment longer she might keep the shuffling Negro in sight.

When the Negro had passed from sight the woman re-turned to her dishes. There were only four plates and four cups and saucers and an odd assortment of pans and bowls. These were the dirty dishes of yesterday's meals and break-fast this morning. She washed her own dishes only every second day and then with distaste because she earned her liv-ing as a cleaning woman.

When she had dried the last cup carefully she put it away in the cabinet above the sink. Her mind was not with what she was doing. She was thinking of the Negro. She was see-ing him still as she had while she watched him shuffling up the street, her eyes secret and hostile.

If he ever looked up, she thought. Several times she had

felt the impulse to wave her dishcloth or make some kind of motion to get his attention, but she had never been able to bring herself to do it. She only stared at him, dropping her eyes in a fury of panic if he turned his head toward the house lest he raise his eyes and meet her own.

She was afraid. What might he read in her eyes? But she resented his indifference, too.

Like I wasn't worth looking at, she thought, wringing the dishrag in her big red soap-crinkled hands with such angry vehemence threads in the fabric gave.

If ever, she thought. But she had never been able to think exactly what the nature of the contingency was, whether or not she would recognize it, or what she would do. She avoided clarifying the thought to herself by momentarily shrouding the image of the Negro in the dull, smothering cloth of resentment.

My mercy! the woman exclaimed, looking at the dial of the cheap alarm clock that was an exact replica of the Negro Dandelion's though she was not aware of this, and grabbed the old fringed shawl she wore tied about her head. Unless she hurried she would be late reporting for work at the Brophys' where she swept and dusted the whole house and had to take particular care in cleaning the great grand piano in the parlor at which Mary Brophy gave piano lessons to the children of Tilden.

And I a white woman, she thought in a final flare of rage against the Negro Dandelion. She had equated their tasks in her mind and found them the same except that his were a little the more menial.

# V

THE STREET that ran by Dandelion's house was a street of no name. It lost its character as a street a hundred yards beyond, becoming suddenly a winding dirt road that idled into the countryside. It was a poor street, pocked with potholes; the sidewalks on either side were overgrown with grass and weeds and blackberry briars that in their ripe season dropped windfalls to stain the concrete the color of spilled wine. In the direction of the open fields and woods beyond the abruptly ended street there were no other houses in sight. Inward toward the heart of the town poor dwellings, mostly uninhabited, were sprinkled on either side.

There was still no light when Dandelion reached the street. As he walked he could feel the mass of the approaching day weighing against his flesh, and he raised his head as if to worship also when somewhere in the hills toward the place where the farmer Abraham lived a rooster crowed, saluting the unseen sun.

The first drift of day swept through the town as Dandelion approached the house of the white woman, and passed, running the gantlet of her hidden eyes. By the time he had passed her house all the westward mountains were fired with light.

And rising above the hills the sun itself discovered the Negro limping along the street on the outer fringe of the town, not far from where he set out. His walk was a rustling shuffle; it was a preposterous gait and rock at which he moved but the sun took no note of his defection, for it discovered it not to itself but to any eyes that watched him moving along the street. His preposterous walk served to advance him slowly, but on this morning of August the nineteenth his lame legs bore him swiftly enough, since within the compass of the rounding day he moved to meet his death.

# VI

THE PLACE of the farmer Abraham was situated on a table-
land, a gently sloped pause of earth between the hills behind
and the flat plain upon which the town was built. From there
he had a clear view of the country below him. From this
height he had often noted how the darkness that lay over
Tilden of mornings when the surrounding landscape was
whole with light shrank slowly and became wrinkled and
flabby as it grew less, like a drying blob of discolored phlegm
spit into a declivity by a giant.

Now Abraham stood outside his house in the straw-colored
morning and looked down the incline of earth toward Tilden.
He had nothing to do before breakfast for he entrusted the
chores about the farm to his sons. Or rather they had inherited them on coming of age to do men's work, as Abraham
had inherited the chores from his own father. There was a
wedge-like sound of an ax blade in wood, and a little farther
off the indistinct sound of a boy's voice talking to the farmyard animals. On a farm, Abraham was thinking, animals
become personalities and if one is good-spirited he speaks to
them kindly, often with humor, and as often with the indrawn inflections of love. So a son of Abraham was speaking
to a lot full of calves.

He was a seed, thought Abraham, in a pod of my flesh. For the farmer thinks in terms of planting and harvest and in that cycle of always-analogy, mostly of planting; the harvest is the Lord's.

Abraham knew already what he was to do for the day. He had three plows that needed sharpening. When he thought of this images of the plows existed in his mind, and there he tested again their dull points worn blunt in the tilling of the soil. He could also picture in his mind the time when he would have been to the blacksmith's and could test the renewed points of the plows and feel them clean sharp against the palms of his finger-tips.

He had not been to the blacksmith's yet, and wanted to postpone the thought of having been there. He wanted to look forward to the journey. In his mind he assembled the three plows, a bull-tongue plow for opening the earth, a half-twister for covering seed, and a sweep for cultivating, as he would do later, for there was no need to assemble the plows until after breakfast when he would be ready to go. Being an orderly man, Abraham knew exactly where to lay his hands on them, and he would pick them up on his way by the barn on setting out for Tilden.

Abraham knew that he would have no need of the plows again until spring. This was August. This was the time between laying-by and the beginning of harvest. He meant to have the plows sharpened now and hold them in readiness against the need of them in a new season. He thought of the time when winter would hold sterile dominion over the earth. When he thought of this there was a voice which spoke in his mind. It was an old voice of many inflections. What, in sum, it said to Abraham was that he might have no need of the plows when spring came again.

When he heard the voice, Abraham shook his head which was square-shaped and crowned with short cropped hair the color of soot and salt. Lines appeared around his mouth and puckered his whole face which was weathered brown and creased like old leather. He was past middle age and it was out of the wisdom bequeathed him by time and experience that he knew an answer to what the voice said.

Should he be part of the earth when spring came, his sons would need plows to stir to renewed life that part of him desert in the dust.

He named then his sons in his mind: John, Isaac, Richard, Ranse, Alfred, Fedder, Frank. As he named his sons the face to which each name belonged appeared in his mind and then disappeared like faces of a squad of soldiers counting off.

Just as Abraham turned to enter the house the sun struck in the yard and flamed there like a bolt of lightning inextricably caught in the place of its striking.

# VII

A QUARTER of a mile beyond the white woman's box-square house the street of no name on which the Negro Dandelion walked entered Maple Street, street of the best houses in Tilden, which ran all the way through the town, serving as its central axis. Dandelion was always glad to see the bustle along Maple Street. Not until he reached it did the morning begin. Along it was a world different in kind from the world of quiet and threat that lay along the street of no name. The eyes that watched him on Maple Street were frank and superior and without threat. He sometimes thought that this was more his world than the section of town that had been permitted to him and his people who wore the face of darkness before he had been left the single inhabitant of niggertown.

I ain't think about it, Dandelion said to himself. He craned his head and looked into the sky toward the east. The red fire of day was kindled there and it warmed him to think of the sun. But in spite of himself he thought of his people and again he smelt the sweat and fear of them as they cowered in their houses in the time before the Exodus.

Because of a little white stuff, Dandelion thought. He remembered with a sudden violent wrench at his stomach the image of Hester McCracken as he had seen her lying nude and dead in a ditch. He had been among those impressed by the sheriff to remove the body, had been forced to touch her and lift her from where she had fallen across a stone at the bottom of the ditch; her torso elevated by the stone rose suggestively above her swollen legs flung out in a loose final abandonment. There was a look of idiot delight on her face as if she had found death the most ravishing lover of all.

She had been a whore. Aah, Dandelion said aloud in an expulsion of breath that cleaned his mind by blowing the term out of his mouth. A short while before her death she had been delivered of a half-black boy child. A midwife delivered her and soon the birth was the common knowledge of the town.

It was reported that more than one white man swore that no white bitch could make a fool out of him with a lousy god-damn nigger.

Somebody was cuckolded by a nigger boy, Dandelion thought. At the memory he allowed himself a short high-pitched peal of bitter laughter. Then his face grew serious again and he humbled it into its customary obsequious lines lest it betray him.

Naah, Dandelion said to himself. Then in his mind he again read the note that had been pinned to the half-black child's blanket when it was found in a basket on Elder Pate's doorstep on the morning following the discovery of Hester McCracken's death. The minister of Tilden's Negro church carried the note from house to house and each man read it, and Dandelion last because he was lame and somehow in default even among his own people.

The note was spelled out in the desperately articulate idiom of a near illiterate. It read:

Dear Reverend
    The mother of this baby has been took care of. If its daddy will give hisself up we will hang him to a limb and let the rest of you be. If he don't we will hang all the nigger men to a limb one at a time as that way we will be sure of taking care of its daddy too.

The note was unsigned except for an ominous splash of red ink which looked remarkably like blood.

But I ain't think about that, Dandelion said to himself as he approached Maple Street. Yet his mind went of its own volition to the Exodus of his people.

The Reverend Elder Pate went among his flock and exhorted but no one, man nor boy, came forth to claim fatherhood of the half-black child and the scapegoat that was secret among them bloated on the fear of the guilty until it grew out of size and became them all.

The second night after Hester McCracken's death a file of cars drove slowly through niggertown and wherever there was a black face at a window or behind a door watching, the fear that had been born of Elder Pate's reading of the note sprang full blown into obsession. It became ritual and desperate. From that time no colored person dared go into Tilden for supplies and finally all began to starve, so they bundled what of their belongings they could carry into suitcases and bedsheets and marched in a body and with processional solemn movement up the dark street by Dandelion's house and into the country and the friendly night.

So they had stolen in silence and stealth from their houses

to the edge of town, but they had not left Tilden without plaint or token of their going. Once beyond the abruptly ended street, in reach of the woods to hide, they turned and shouted a volley of curses back into the town.

He had heard them as he lay awake in his own bed in the hours beyond midnight drenched in the sweat of his own fear. He heard them invoking loud, profane damnation upon the town and its people. After a while the curses took on a vulgar holiday tone. Then a strong tenor bequeathed Hester McCracken's bastard to the town of Tilden; then there was laughter followed by a silence that was not broken by the same voices ever.

That had been the Exodus. He could not go with his people because he was lame. He did not know if they had ever reached a promised land.

# VIII

Aunt Angelicia, whom the Negro Dandelion called Miss Angeley, was a woman of considerable wealth, a widow and of such a motherly interfering nature as makes some women acquire the title of aunt without consideration of relatedness. In Aunt Angelicia's case, however, the title was amply justified by a raft of nephews and nieces. Her particular charge and choice of them all was her brother-in-law's oldest child, a girl at once shy and aggressive, named Rhoda.

Aunt Angelicia was beginning to be old. Her head which she held by habit at a regal tilt, as if balancing a crown, was now white, not the dirty white or the pepperish white which women despise but the pure white of marble or of snow with which they are content, if not proud. Her face was lined with deep wrinkles but it was a strong face, the planes of it willful and uncompromising, like a man's.

While the Negro Dandelion was still hobbling along the street of no name, Aunt Angelicia stood at her back kitchen door ringed by a semicircle of tawny, expectant cats, and watched day breaking along Maple Street.

Before her in the dawn light misting to heat she saw the garden wavering to view. Over the lawn the great red cannas seemed to burn, their boiling flames contained in craters of green leaves. The garden was walled on all four sides and

33

enclosed two acres of finely set grass and flowers and shrubs set in semiformal patterns over the lawn. The house itself occupied the corner of the garden in the angle formed by the intersection of Maple and Center Streets. In the far corner of the garden with its back set close to the wall that ran along Center Street was an open-fronted summerhouse built of field stone and roofed with red tile. It had been built to hold the garden tools and for storage, but now, summer and winter, it was given over to the cats.

At the first sounds from the kitchen the cats had moved up through the garden from their beds in the summerhouse as if drawn out from there by the woman's gaze. She watched them as they came with heavy somnolent tread, their urge to hunt shining, slumberous but fixed, from their quick eyes. She always fed them to satiety and they grew fat and as different from the ordinary prowling house cat as if they belonged to a different species, a species closer to the tiger that steals in great-padded silence through his runs of straw.

All across the garden she had watched them. Now she opened the door and they entered single file. As they fed at the basins already set out by Nettie, the kitchen help, their tails waved above the floor of the kitchen, interwove and caressed each other, moving in the air like a nest of furry snakes.

Aunt Angelicia watched the feeding cats without comment. She often owned as many as fifteen or more and neither she nor anyone in Tilden thought it was strange that she should keep so many. She was able to keep them and it seemed to Tilden that she was only doing right by the homeless when she adopted the stray cats of the town. The owners of unwanted cats thought she was unaware of how they brought them quietly by night and dropped them over the wall of the garden by the summerhouse.

It was only that she said nothing; cats had so long been a part of her household they seemed as indispensable as Nettie the cook, or Dandelion on whom she had come to depend to look after the cleaning of the summerhouse where the cats slept.

When the cats had finished eating and she had let them out into the garden again, she became aware that one of the cats was missing. A great yellow-striped male cat had not fed with the others.

"Tawm?" she called out into the garden.

The night before she had dreamed of the cat. His stature was enlarged in the dream and she saw him like a marble figure brooding fixed and frozen in a posture of spitting pride high over the lawn near the summerhouse.

Aunt Angelicia stepped outside and stood in the shadow of the house looking out over the flowering cannas. Her lips were always pursed, as if molded about the sound of the letter Q, which gave her face a deceptive quality of thoughtfulness. She seemed always to ponder some weighty matter. This was not true. Aunt Angelicia was not a thoughtless woman yet she accepted for her own the mores of her group without undue examination to determine whether they were right or wrong, just or unjust, merciful or unkind. She wore the status quo as a cloak, and the cloak changed little in style, only gathering a frill here and there or dropping a pleat or a pucker, alterations that could be effected without change in the basic cut of the garment. If at her age she was somewhat out of style she was not so maliciously. Each generation can afford but its single cloak.

"Tawm?" Aunt Angelicia called. Yet her mind was not

on the cat. As soon as she had gone into the garden a figure rose from among the flower beds and began to walk slowly over the shorn grass. The figure was gowned in tulle and came forward with a ceremonious stateliness of movement. Somewhere there must be the sound of an organ but Aunt Angelicia could not hear it peal.

There was something about the appearance of the figure so suggestive of the promise and event of marriage that for a moment Aunt Angelicia's mind was turned back to the time when she herself stood in the cool interior of the church and whispered the indelible vows. That was in the weather of a time long past. Almost fifty summers had blown and faded since she approached the altar with a man old enough to be her father. Aunt Angelicia had always planned to marry a man rich enough to give her a house with white-columned front porch and a walled garden with an entrance flanked by wide flaring masonry wings crowned by twin stone urns. To achieve her ends she had had to marry a man already middle-aged, a lawyer and later a circuit judge. Remembering Judge Harlock's intermittent ardor she thought it somewhat strange that their union had not been blessed by children. She had wanted children.

The childless woman stared out over the garden where the cannas flamed in the August morning. She felt old and tired and a little cheated because she had no son to carry on the family name. She had wanted especially a male child, for she considered her husband a very distinguished person and of accomplishments worthy of perpetuation through a son.

As she thought of the dead Judge Harlock her face began to soften. It was not that she blamed him. On the contrary she considered her marriage at twenty to the distinguished-looking gray-haired lawyer who soon after their union

36

became Judge Harlock a decided success. He had given her wealth and position, and the white-columned house and the walled garden, and, even to the strictest specification of her dreams, the twin stone urns.

"Tawm, Tawm?" Aunt Angelicia called. It was almost as if the great male cat was her child and lost. The dead tones of her voice hung in the morning air an instant and were absorbed into the heated distance between her and the garden's edge.

Since she had no children of her own Aunt Angelicia took an active interest in the children of others, especially in the children of her husband's brother who had never prospered.

A ne'er-do-well, apostrophe and all, thought Angelicia all but contemptuously.

There were six of these children, all born since Judge Harlock's death, and all at Angelicia's expense, for the judge's brother could never manage to pay the doctor's bills. During the judge's lifetime and his tenure on the bench some small political job had always been found for his brother. When Judge Harlock died the man who succeeded him had relatives of his own to consider.

Of her six nieces and nephews it was the oldest, the girl Rhoda, which Aunt Angelicia cherished most. She thought of her care of Rhoda in the ancient figure of taking the child under her wing. She did this partly because she liked to extend the figure and think how it was an ample wing that gave the child shelter, a wing feathered with stocks and bonds plus investments drawing good rates of interest from Mr. Darlington's bank. Though Rhoda was strong-willed and at times revolted against her aunt's too tender care, Angelicia was patient. She held her peace and knew that it was because Rhoda was still a child. Aunt Angelicia could be objective enough about it to realize that the atmosphere under her wing could be too close, but there would come times in the life of Rhoda when it would afford a good place to hide. Too, as the child grew older she would come to appreciate more and more the sheen of the feathers.

The sun was now full above the hills in the east. The sunlight came straight down Maple Street like a presence of gold. One could mark its progress from stone to stone along the street, as if it were a flow of golden water or of a more viscous liquid, like oil. Soon the rays struck Aunt Angelicia full in the face and she lifted her hand and shaded her eyes against the probing sunlight.

The figure gowned in tulle moved without speech or sound over the shorn grass. Where it had stepped there was no imprint of feet for it was without substance. It existed only in Aunt Angelicia's mind. She was not sure when she had first visualized the figure. It was not before her husband's death. She believed it had been after the rancored meeting when Rhoda's father agreed that the child should come and go to her aunt's house as she liked and that Aunt Angelicia should assume the burden of the child's education. He would not agree for the child to come and live with Angelicia as her own. Some parents are selfish, thought Aunt Angelicia.

Now the figure was close to Aunt Angelicia. It stood poised before a bank of blooming cannas in an attitude of expectancy, as if waiting to be joined by another who was tardy, who had been inexplicably detained.

# IX

Aunt Angelicia's constant dream of the figure in the tulle gown was broken in upon now by the presence of the Negro Dandelion as he came shuffling in from the street to clean the cat house, as he did every morning. She scarcely noticed him. He rarely paused on his way to the cat house even if she happened to be outside in the garden. But this morning he did not go on directly. He came shuffling near her and when he was a few feet away he stopped and held his hat in his hands.

"Miss Angeley?" Dandelion said.

"Yes, Dandy?" she said.

"If I could have a quarter," Dandelion said tentatively. "If you could let me have a quarter."

"A quarter, Dandelion?"

"Yessum."

Aunt Angelicia stared off into the garden, the fantasy she always wove in her mind broken for a moment by the Negro's request. The figure gowned in tulle had disappeared among the fires of the canna beds. It faded from her vision, at first receding like someone backing away and then it became a convolution of whirling light that circled inward upon itself and disappeared in a wink of brilliance. She was almost angry with the Negro for disturbing her dream, though she had been expecting him, had been waiting for him as she stood at the door ringed by the expectant cats.

"We'll discuss it later, Dandy," she said. She moved before him into the garden. He could tell nothing from her face. Her pursed lips gave her whole face a thoughtful cast. She was thinking, but he could not tell what she was thinking.

"Tawm?" Aunt Angelicia called as she walked on into the garden. "That cat hasn't shown himself all morning," she said to Dandelion. "I can't imagine where he is hiding."

"Nawm," he said.

"I suppose he *is* hiding," she said as if any other supposition were utterly incredible.

"Yessum."

"See if Tawm is in the shed when you clean it."

"Yessum," Dandelion said.

She gave him a broom like those used by street sweepers, and he shuffled on across the grass still wet with dew toward the summerhouse where the cats slept. He turned once to look at Aunt Angelicia to see if he could tell whether or not she was going to let him have the quarter. He could tell nothing.

She forgot it already, he thought.

The cannas flicked red-flame shadows against his black skin as he passed.

As Aunt Angelicia walked on into the garden the vision reshaped itself in her mind. The figure was before her again as if it came from hiding from behind the tall cannas, and the cannas themselves grew in her mind and not in the garden. The first identifiable property of the vision was the gown of tulle. She had worn it herself once, on her wedding day, but in the fantasy she was not wearing the gown. She dreamed it upon the form of Rhoda, her niece, and discovered her wearing the gown toward the marriage altar, walking slowly in the hushed expectancy of the promise and event of marriage by the side of her groom. The groom in these fantasies she wove about the marriage of her niece was not always the same person. On this morning of August she saw beside her niece the dark boy Farley, son of the professor of History at Tilden High, grown to manhood and beautiful in his maturity as he was in his now youth. More and more often now the figure beside the tulle-gowned Rhoda moving to the imagined music of the organ that all but fanned the canna leaves was that of the dark boy. She was beginning to think now that this had significance beyond the dream. It was as if the figure of the boy had entered the dream of his own accord and not through her summons, and this often enough to make his presence there an omen. Once or twice the figure had been that of the blond boy Jonathan but his presence there somehow violated the integrity of the dream, and each time she had cast him out.

She thought again of the cat.

"Tawm?" Aunt Angelicia called. A dozen cats of different breeds and colors came tumbling. They arched their backs and rubbed against her legs as she moved; looking down it seemed to the woman that she too had feet of fur.

She considered the cats, her lips pursed. Now where could that cat be, she thought, naming those present to herself. When she had finished naming the cats tumbling about her feet, she had left the name of the missing cat, and she called it aloud into the garden:

"Tawm!"

The Negro Dandelion came toward her from the summerhouse.

"Dandelion," she said, "I thought you were cleaning the shed." She had forgotten to mark time and it seemed only a moment ago that the Negro had entered the yard.

"Yessum," Dandelion said. "Yessum, Miss Angeley, but I done clean up where the cats been. I'd . . ."

"*Angelicia*, Dandy, how many times must I tell you?"

"Yessum."

"Did you see Tawm?"

"Nawm, Miss Angeley. Ain't seen Mr. Tawm since yesterday morning. He there with the rest of them then."

"Tawm's gone," Aunt Angelicia said, her voice incredulous. "Dandy?"

"Yessum, Miss Angeley."

"Tawm's gone, do you suppose . . . ?"

"Nawm, Miss Angeley."

Aunt Angelicia continued to look at him, not releasing him though he had already denied the question made explicit in her eyes.

"Nawm, Miss Angeley, not the way he fixed," the Negro said. He squirmed in embarrassment.

"Well, I suppose not," Aunt Angelicia said. She lifted her head to its regal tilt, her white hair shining, and looked out beyond Dandelion over the garden. "Look out for him, Dandy. Ask if anyone has seen him. He might be just strayed, you know."

"Yessum, Miss Angeley."

"Angelicia," she said, patiently correctional. Her eyes had left him, gone out into the garden.

"Miss Angeley."

"What is it now, Dandelion?"

"If you could let me have a quarter."

"A quarter, Dandelion? You know that *Friday* is payday.

How many people pay you on Friday as I do so you will have money to spend for your own needs on Saturday?"

"Nawm, they don't pay me like you do, Miss Angeley. But I'd mighty like to have a quarter."

"And Tawm's gone, Dandy." She said it as if she accused him of negligence that had made possible the escape of the great yellow striped cat that had stepped among the others with the proud disinterested authority of a chief eunuch in a harem.

"Yessum," Dandelion said. He could not bring himself to mention that he had no snuff in the presence of Aunt Angelicia's grief and concern with the disappearance of the great emasculated cat. He began to move away from the woman, shuffling, watching the strong lined face of Aunt Angelicia who looked out over the garden where a half-dozen cats sunned or frolicked or chased butterflies in and out among the fires of the blooming cannas.

He was a little hurt by Aunt Angelicia's evasion of his request for a quarter against his week's wages not yet due but he laid it to her grief over the loss of the cat and was mollified. Yet his longing for snuff was as great as ever.

I dreamt that, he thought as he neared the small gate that let out upon the street at the rear of the house. He would come soon to Miss Ella's place. Perhaps she would spare him a quarter.

He was about to shuffle through the gate when Rhoda came skipping through it, her white dress flaring, its pleats like petals of flowers blooming downward from the stem of her small tight waist. The niece of Aunt Angelicia gave him a little spontaneous courtesy, a slight bend and nod of recognition. Then she was beyond him and he turned to watch her. Her Aunt Angelicia was by now deep in the garden near the open-shedded summerhouse built close to the wall. Rhoda stopped suddenly and her face shut into a mask and she stood arrested near one of the canna beds, watching her aunt.

I dreamt it all, Dandelion thought, reading in the girl's frozen face the fate of the cat. He carried the vision of the arrested girl forward with him as he shuffled onto the street. But soon the vision of her was lost in his desire for a taste of snuff.

# X

WHEN breakfast was over the farmer Abraham prepared to go into the town. This preparation consisted of changing into a clean shirt and overalls and shining his scuffed shoes.

The voice of Sarah, his wife, followed Abraham all through the house as he changed.

"Your clean shirt is on the second shelf," she said, as if he did not know that his clean shirts had always been kept on the second shelf of the clothes press for almost forty years.

Abraham said nothing to his wife beyond asking vaguely, as he always did.

"Is there anything?"

"Nothing," Sarah said as habitually, totting in her mind the store of her provisions to see if there was anything lacking. "But you might bring a box of soda and a bit of salt."

"What else?" Abraham said, for he had learned long ago that Sarah's nothings always prefaced the compiling of a long list of needs.

"A box of grits and a spool of thread. I need some cloves for pickling. And let's see."

"See," Abraham said. He was at the door.

"A darning needle," Sarah said. "The one which sewed the speyed gilt is rusted."

"All right," Abraham said. "I am going now."

The voice of Sarah followed him through the door. It was a patient voice and otherwise without color, like Sarah herself. No one but Abraham knew all the unsuspected strength that was in Sarah's pale being. He seemed scarcely to hear the voice, yet he heard every syllable clearly, and heeded each. The voice said last, "Be careful now." It seemed an odd thing to say to a man going leisurely to the blacksmith shop. Yet Sarah always advised him to be careful and he had learned enough respect for the unexpected and unforeseen not to be contemptuous of her advice.

When he came from the hallway of the barn where he picked up the plows to be sharpened, Abraham could see the town, now bathed in light, lying below him and he began to cast back in his mind to bring together all the fragments of its history which he knew.

The town itself.

Tilden grew by accretion from a small cluster of houses into a municipality that sprawled over the flat plain to the extent of a mile in any direction from a point on the town square. The nucleus of the town had been an inn, a gristmill and a forge situated in three of the four angles formed by two roads that crossed each other as precisely as bisected lines on a surveyor's map. Bart's Creek, named for the original miller, flowed south parallel to the north-south trace until it reached the point of intersection with the east-west trace, where it made a turn as if to outflank the road farther on and flowed westward. The creek was too gentle in its fall to turn the water wheel, and Bart had built a dam of stone across its width and diverted the stream into the race that fed the bucketed wheel. Long after the miller was dead and the mill fallen into disrepair and disuse, this impounded water was known as Bart's Millpond. It slowly filled with silt, and willows and cattails grew in the marshy edges, and green frogs populated the placid shores and cried with basso voices on sultry and rain-washed summer nights. The pond had also been frequented by small boys who came there in summer to swim until the water became so shallow there was not enough depth to drown their naked middles on the approach of passers-by, so out of modesty they finally quit it.

Abraham thought how a man named Anders had established a forge shortly after Bart built his gristmill at the turn of the stream that later bore his name. Anders had settled in the country close by and established a farm which he left to the management of his big lusty sons while he worked at the smithy's trade. His selection of the location for the forge was not without logic. Farmers from the locality brought their grain to be ground at Bart's Mill by wagon and on horseback, and if no horse had cast a shoe and no wagon had sprung a wheel in the deep ruts of the ill-kept road, many a farmer saved himself time and future trouble by having his mount newly shod or some needed repair made on his wagon while waiting his turn at the mill.

Anders was a strong man, and men liked the way he lifted a horse's foot with authority and kept it clamped between his great knees until, the hoof trimmed and honed, the last nail securing a shoe was driven home. Soon Anders' fame spread and he was brought the spirited stable and saddle stallions and the quiet geldings and the pregnant mares to be shod. Many a colt that was shod for the first time by the

47

smith grew old and died wearing shoes shaped on the ringing anvil of Anders' forge.

As Bart's fortunes prospered so did Anders', and then as
Anders' fortunes prospered so did Bart's. For farmers bringing a horse to be shod brought also a turn of grain to be
ground while the shoeing was done. The two men became
fast friends and visited each other of Sundays, as if they did
not associate intimately every day of the week, and their
children intermarried.

Hefting them in his hand, Abraham thought how a
descendant of Bart and Anders would hammer the plows to
a proper edge on the old anvil of Anders' forge and temper
them in water held in a half-barrel as old as the forge itself,
for the forge remained in use though the town had grown
away from it and left it stranded on Tilden's decaying edge.

But the impetus that pushed the town northeastwards
from the crossroads, leaving the disused mill and the aging
forge in its wake, was not a sudden force, and when Bart's
oldest daughter married Anders' second son there was still
nothing at the crossroads but the mill and the forge facing
each other across the east-west trace.

It was about this time, as Abraham knew from the telling
of an ancestor, a man now dark in Abraham's memory while
his report lived on, that a man named Tilden stopped at the
forge to have his horse shod and walked into the center of
the crossroads and looked each way up and down the four
prongs.

"By God," said Tilden, "it might be the center of the
world for all that a man can tell different from here." He
laughed shortly and the black flowing cloth he wore at his
neck bobbed up and down with his strong laughter.

"Could be," said Anders. "Could be, stranger."

"Stranger?" bristled Tilden. "Melvin Tilden ain't never been a stranger to nobody." He held out his hand, and Anders wiped his own hand on his leather apron and took Tilden's in a fierce grip.

"Anders," the smith said.

"A hand for a damn good smith," Tilden said. "It's a wonder you ever need a vise."

The smith grunted.

"Center of the world," said Tilden. "Who owns the land across the trace?"

"I own it," Anders said.

Tilden fiddled with his neck cloth, which the dark man of Abraham's blood had eyed without favor, for the men that frequented the forge and the mill never wore such, not even to church with their Sunday best.

"Would you sell it?" Tilden asked, indicating the land in the southeast angle of the crossroads with a sweep of his big arm.

"I would," Anders said.

"Then hell, man, it's as good as sold."

"As good as sold," agreed Anders, "if the price is right."

"The price will be right," Tilden said. "It will be of your asking."

"Right enough, then," Anders said. "Might a man ask what you want with the land?"

"I'll build an inn."

The man of Abraham's blood, perhaps it had been his grandfather, had known Anders and Tilden both and it was his report and not his own memory that pictured to Abraham the establishment of the inn. The opening had been an

49

occasion with liquor and dancing and laughter and brawl-
ing. Abraham remembered his ancestor telling and telling
of it with repetition of the minutest detail in the manner of
the very old.

Tilden named his inn The Traveler's Rest. He remained
and became a local politician and finally won a seat in the
state senate. He had had ambitions for the governorship but
could never muster quite enough support among the cotton
interests of the state to win the office.

After the building of the inn, travelers, stopping over-
night, began to turn settlers and make homes in the locality,
and soon the crossroads became a town.

When he had gone a little way beyond the bench of earth
on which his own farm was, Abraham stopped thinking of
Tilden, the town, which was now out of sight and his mind
was on a field. In his mind's eye the field was green with
summer. It was at the shadowing time, just before the fall
of night, and no one was in the field. But all day men and
children and now and again a woman bringing water, had
moved back and forth over the field in the act of cultivating
it, bringing it to fruit.

First the blade, Abraham thought, but wait. Before the
blade the seed and before the seed the plow and harrow and
the labor of man and beast. After the blade the stalk and the
time of cultivation culminating in the full and perfect yield,
fruit and seed. This was the way it was, and for moments
he walked lost in the contemplation of the whole cycle of
growth.

Summer was on the fields, green with the blood of life,
through which Abraham walked and beheld them ripening
to harvest.

He dreamed the intervention of winter.

Then in his mind it was spring again, and he looked upon a field. It was prepared for the planting, the soil had been broken by the plow. It was the proper season. There was warmth in the soil. The furrow was open. What he saw was a barren field. A field perfect in all its properties, but barren.

You must put the seed in, Abraham thought. It is the seed which is germinal. And immediately there was in his mind the roster of his sons' names: John, Isaac, Richard, Ranse, Alfred, Fedder, Frank.

By now Abraham had reached the edge of Tilden. Before him he saw the Negro Dandelion's house, empty, unshuttered, standing a little way back from the street. There was no life about the place except for a few scrawny chickens that scratched in a lot made of sagging wire strung upon trees that grew in a sparse grove to the left of the house.

"Dandy," Abraham called. He was of a mind to pass the time of day with the Negro, but there was no reply from the house. He stood a moment in the street before Dandelion's house and looked about him. Up and down the street on either side stood the empty shanties that had comprised niggertown before all the colored people had left suddenly in the night.

And left their curses upon the town, thought Abraham.

And left as Tilden's ward Hester McCracken's bastard, a whinny-voiced idiot who had a purplish-black skin, in color like the face of a strangulated man.

To balance and outweigh the vision of the misshapen half-black child, Abraham thought of his own strong sons, each of them sturdy and straight and the flesh of them barley-gold in color.

Abraham was still thinking of his sons when he reached

Maple Street and saw Dandelion shuffling along a little way before him, moving with his grotesque stride from the widow Angelicia's toward the spinster Miss Ella's, and toward his death.

# XI

BEFORE THE sudden sight of the Negro Dandelion and her aunt about their business with the cats arrested the flouncing motion of the girl Rhoda in Angelicia's garden the boy Farley woke in his house on Maple Street, which was the street of day because it lay east and west and each morning the sun came up it like a returning native dressed in fantastic robes from the fabled East. On waking Farley stared at the walls of his room which were four and usually hung here and there with trophies of his boyhood and waited for his dream to fade. Waking or sleeping his dream was the same. It was of the blond boy Jonathan, his friend. Sometime during each day he was in the presence of Jonathan himself, but their togetherness was cleft, by a hinder, by a halt, by a spread of light or of air. In the dark and the dream all things wore a unity, either of the darkness or of the dream, and there was no impediment of flesh between his hands and the small bones of Jonathan, white as sticks of ash but sheened like pearl.

It was already day. Outside the noise of the wakened town moving to work sounded on the long street. As he lay listening another sound came to the boy. It was that of his mother's voice from deep in the house, telling him to wake. Since he was awake already he felt no compulsion to answer his mother. Instead he gave his attention to the sounds of passing. From where he was the street was not in view, and as he heard the sound of feet against the pavement he envisioned

53

the morning movement of people going toward the center of town as a stream because of its one-way set of flow. The individuals who in reality moved forever separate in his mind merged each into each, their lives became life and it flowed a river over the bedrock of stone which was the morning street. Some of its current caught in the neighboring houses and some flowed on into the center of town and was diverted through doors into cavernous buildings. Some of the life that flowed by his house entered the bank and was dammed there until three o'clock each day. Some of it flowed to the grocery stores, and more of it flowed to the shops and factories on the far side of town where it churned underground until evening, when the current was reversed and all life flowed outward from the center of town and was diverted into the doors of dwellings. Only now and then, morning or evening, did the flow of life, narrowed by the confines of the street, widen at either side of the town and continue into the limitless spaces beyond.

From this flow, which was amorphous, he could separate entities, units, individuals, and make them singular again. He did this by deciphering the telegraphy of tread. There was the groceryman who had a limp which broke the rhythm of his stride over a bar of pause, yet established it in a distinct pattern of its own unmistakable to the boy's accustomed ear. Each morning the groceryman passed early, going to his store to set it in order before the opening hour. Somewhat later the boy Farley would hear the heavy tread which marked the ponderous passage of Mr. Darlington, the banker, along the street. Mr. Darlington, who was Mr. Money to the boy, lived three blocks from Farley's own door, in the town's most impressive house as befitted its richest man, and regularly except on those rare occasions when he felt indisposed the banker walked the distance from his house to the bank, nodding or speaking to everyone he met.

Mr. Darlington was great of bulk and dignified, like the façade of his own bank. The boy Farley imagined he saw inside that great-bulked body the accouterments of the bank's interior. Through the teller windows of the eyes he saw the adding machines and computers, and the safe which was the brain. Inside the safe there was contained money, stacks of it, green and denominated in monstrous figures, and spilling piles of silver. There was only money in the safe for there was room for nothing else. Farley saw how the greetings and the words of others were turned into bills and deposited in Mr. Darlington's safe. These he would pass out again as loans to others through the little wicket gate of his mouth. And no one failed to greet, or be greeted, on encountering Mr. Darlington as he moved part of the current and flow of life over the bedrock of stone that was diverted into the cavern of the bank. Much of the whole current of life down that street was diverted, seldom or often, into that cavern.

"Farley!" his mother called, giving his name a far and lengthened sound so that he thought at once of the voice of one lost calling through distance and fog. His mother rarely flowed in the current of life down their street. She was contained daily in the cavern of her own house, subterranean, and to her son the sound of her being was muted and quiet like the low murmur of water flowing underground. His mother's was the face of *do this* or *you cannot*, as his father's was that of *I'd advise you, Son*, yet it was a more personal face than his father's. On hearing her voice her face appeared in his mind and the image he had of her did not change though he had had the same image since the beginning of memory.

The passing of the years must have altered, if only slightly, the real face. Neither life nor time flowing altered the image. It was of a young woman's face, oval and delicately humorous but touched with a sadness about the mouth. Her eyes were haunted perpetually by a strangeness, a look compounded of wonder, pain and surprise. When she looked at his father there was nothing but wonder in her gaze, but he imagined that when she looked at him it was with a stare of improbable surprise, as if she entered a room and found one unexpected there. Always, even when he saw the image divorced from the face, he read the involuntary truth of the eyes and finally his own exclusion became witnessed there.

His mother was rarely part of the flow of life down the stone street, but regularly his father rose of mornings and had his coffee and toast, then kissed his wife and stepped out into the eight o'clock current and was borne to the Tilden Library where he was assistant librarian during the summer. During the rest of the year he was professor of English and History at Tilden High. Farley's father was a quiet man whose search was of the sands of Egypt and among the stones of ancient Greece. He was not interested in local politics except as they approximated the politics of Tut, or differed from the machinations known to the Ammonitish kings, which they did not to any great extent. From the rich idiom of his fellows who spoke from the mouths of their Anglo-Saxon forebears he extracted those bits of speech that were twinned in the songs of Lovelace or in the tales and plays of Chaucer and Shakespeare. These he entered in his notebook and from them wrote articles for folklore journals and was paid in contributor's copies.

Now the boy heard his father step from the door onto the street and for moments the clitter-clatter sound of his going came back on the weighted August air. He rose from the bed and went to the window for a view of his father's progress down the street, but he could not see him. He was already hidden from sight by the hanging maple boughs. Once broken from the still mold that was of sleep and established in movement, the boy strode across the room again. His movements were quick and determined and when they brought him before the mirror of his bureau he stopped and looked at his image in the glass.

When he looked in the glass he saw his father young again, for he had inherited the brooding darkness of his father's face. It was as if his father had refined the metal of his own being and poured it into a finer and more symmetrical cast and broken it out afresh.

I am my father, Farley thought. Then he passed in his mind through the door of his father's bedroom into the kitchen and drank a cup of coffee, which he was not allowed as himself. Then rising, he kissed his mother as his wife, the blood draining from his face, and marveled at the cold touch of her lips for his own flesh was always warm. As his father still he rejected the proffered morning paper held in his mother's delicate small hand, and passed by way of the front door into the morning flow of life down Maple Street.

Then he had to abandon his father's being, for he had no idea what his father's life at the library was like. He knew nothing of his father's absorption, and the clean impelling joy of it, in the record of man's stay upon the provident earth. He knew nothing of how his father repatriated all people he met to the kingdom of Thebes and there judged them for courage and courtesy and found them wanting.

When he abandoned his father's being he resumed his own, standing before the mirror still. From impulse he removed his pajama coat and threw it from him and then loosed the cord of the trousers and let them fall to the floor. Seeing his own well-proportioned and perfectly developed body imaged in the mirror from the top of his head to the bulge of his knees there was nothing else to do but greet it in the affirmative. Yes, he said to his body and felt within himself the quiet calm of acceptance. Besides the entity and warren of himself, it was a correspondence map of the body of Jonathan defining the other's shape and marking by symbols of the immutable legend the location of his hidden regions, mysterious and unexplored.

"Farley!" his mother called and he knew that his breakfast was waiting for him in the kitchen and soon he must leave his room which was the quarters of his dream and go into his mother's domain which was cold from the reflections of her arctic face. He gauged the degree of impatience in her voice and knew that unless he went soon she would come to his room and open the door and force him out by the unspoken command of her stiff presence.

Morning is reluctance. In his unwillingness to respond to his mother's call he made the equation. He gathered weight to his thought from all that touched his mind. Outside in the morning air grown stuffy already in the August heat a bird called in a dispirited voice. No bird answered the caller and its skipping notes flew over bars of silence and died and were renewed in a tone of utter weariness. Even the bird, he thought.

Up from the town came the solemn bonging of the clock as it struck an indefinite hour. He missed the count of its striking and knew only that it was morning and summer. Then he heard a light mincing tread upon the sidewalk outside and thought at once of Miss Ella, the willowy spinster who kept a small bookstore on the square of the town. He saw her in his mind as she looked fluttering about in her store, her hands at the height of her shoulders fanning like small bird wings, her fingers moving as if she could not restrain herself from turning the pages of the books her customers held, inspecting. *Now here*, or *this one*, she was always saying, offering one book after another to tempt the reluctant. He thought of her sometimes as saying, *Now here is a world of words inhabited by people of no body, no breath*. He was sure that Miss Ella preferred the world of words to any other. Where she lived alone near the widening of the world into the limitless country beyond the borders of Tilden, her neat small house bulged with books. The boy Farley often visited her there and found her reading, lost in a word world, touched, he imagined, now and then by the lifeless, weightless hand of a paper hero.

But the passer was not Miss Ella. By the time he had reached the window to look the street was empty, and over the empty street the air brooded, lit with green reflected from the brass sky polished to shining by the wilted mops of trees that moved against it as the winds of August rose and decreased with the sound of air leaking from a damaged bellows. A milk truck clattered into town leaving injured silence in its wake.

While the boy was at the window the memory of two events stirred in him, events having a common denominator, which was time. The first concerned Rhoda, the girl. Each morning of summer Rhoda, accompanied by her Aunt Angelicia, passed down the street to Miss Brophy's house where Rhoda sat on the mahogany bench and had her music lesson. Rhoda was a member of a large family that was poor in the genteel tradition of those who combine poverty with a prominent family name. All the members of that family were poor, except Rhoda. She was not poor because Aunt Angelicia was not poor. Aunt Angelicia insisted on maintaining Rhoda in the manner of the best families. To prevent embarrassment to Rhoda, Aunt Angelicia opened her purse to the other members of the family when they became too hard pressed to continue in dignity. It was because Aunt Angelicia wished it that Rhoda went each morning and sat in the parlor of Miss Brophy's house and had her music lesson.

Under Miss Brophy's tutoring Rhoda had progressed to Bach. That morning when she stopped at his house, as she often did while his mother and Aunt Angelicia gossiped, she was carrying under her arm *The Well Tempered Clavichord*. He took the music from her and turned the pages.

"Batch," he said, "it's by Batch."

"Not Batch, stupid," Rhoda said, "it's Bok."

"Batch," he said again, laughing. "It looks like Batch."

"It's Bok," she said seriously, and her voice had a slight inflection of superiority which irked him. Suddenly he had an impulse and he put his face so close to hers he could feel the emanation of her warmth.

"I can give you Bok," he said in a sultry voice, and she understood him at once. She shrieked and dropped her eyes and fled blushing into the hall.

"Bok," he called after her without reference to the composer, but she had regained her poise and when she marched off with Aunt Angelicia the dignity she had assumed to compensate for the shame of the proposal couched in his voice stiffened her back. Afterwards when she would pass there was a new intimacy in the look that passed between them. Sometime, he promised himself each time he saw her, not quite knowing the conditions of his promise.

# THE HAWK AND THE SUN

When the girl was gone that morning another figure appeared on the street. A boy of his own age pedaled by on his bicycle. The boy looked up as he passed and lifted a bare, sunburned arm in greeting and pedaled on his way. He casually beheld the boy. He saw him out of sight and then his attention was claimed by some other matter. Later, when he remembered, it was not Rhoda's but that other morning face that lived in his mind, the perfect cast of features, the quick smile and, shining like ripe wheat in the sun, the crown of so-blond hair.

Thinking of these two, for a moment his mind brushed yesterday's interim behind the summerhouse. The atmosphere was tight and close with the presence and yielding of the girl. But somehow the vision was redeemed because it contained also the blond boy Jonathan's bright, unimpeachable face.

Farley turned again into his room and his eyes fell on a cabinet in the corner where his baseball and catcher's mitt lay neatly in place on top. His baseball bat stood against the cabinet and above it hung his tennis racket. He regarded these emblems of his dearest activities with a frown growing on his face. He took an imaginary swing with the bat, then shook his head, dreaming in the lassitude of heat a less strenuous play. The air inside the room had begun to grow oppressive.

Deep in the house his mother shouted his name. He began to draw on a pair of light khaki trousers, submerging the nakedness of his lower limbs into the tan cloth. When he had donned these he put on a light sport shirt and a pair of sandals.

Before making his way to the kitchen he paused, listening. The bird's voice and his mother's had ceased. For a moment

61

there was nothing but silence. Then he heard the shuffling sound of the Negro Dandelion as he approached from the direction of the corner where Maple Street was intersected by the shabby street of no name on which the Negro lived.

He went to the window and leaned out of it.

"Morning, Mr. Farley," the Negro said.

"Hi," he said.

The Negro bowed slightly as he spoke to Farley. The boy watched him, assessing the bundle of black flesh and crooked bones for its essential difference from himself.

There was nothing except the fact of the Negro's lameness and his obsequious air. He felt the hindrance in the misshapen bones of the black man as he labored up the street toward the east, making a hedging slow progress. It was as if day were an embattled country which he must cross.

# XII

WHEN THE girl Rhoda saw the Negro Dandelion she remembered that she had wakened to a memory of the death of the cat. In her mind she had revoked yesterday, but now at the sight of the Negro and her aunt it lived again. She stood by the tall cannas and looked straight before her toward the summerhouse given over to the cats. Without looking directly at him, she saw the Negro Dandelion retreating from the field of her vision toward Center Street. She saw him bow and disappear. On the left her aunt ringed by the expectant cats moved in her tranced sight. She was moving toward the shed and suddenly she too disappeared, whether behind the shed itself or behind the tall cannas Rhoda had not seen.

I didn't mean to, Rhoda said to herself. Though she avoided looking at it, the shed existed clear in her vision. Behind it she saw the freshly turned oblong in the porous soil that sweated in the shade of the maple boughs.

I hate Jonathan, the girl thought. The harmony of her being disrupted into dissonance at the thought of the blond boy Jonathan and the clear, vivid beauty of his face. Then she thought of the dark boy Farley and three heavy chords of music, as of Bach, dominated and restored to her the harmony of herself.

She moved a step forward and lifted her eyes and looked at the shed. The garden tilted, whirled, spinning the flame of the cannas so they made a circle the color of fire against the garden's blurred green. Then yesterday's concentric hours tightened, the coil of time caught up its slack, and it was today.

She had awakened to a memory of the death of the cat.

To begin it, she thought, and again she saw Farley and Jonathan coming into the garden from Maple Street. It was about nine o'clock and there was the day before them, the long summer day of school vacation, and with a feeling of elation she left the sun parlor and went into the garden to meet them.

"Where are you going?" she said.

"Here," they said as one. They stood shoulder to shoulder facing her, smiling. She moved between them and looked from one to the other.

"What are we going to do?" she said.

"What do you want to do?" Farley said. Jonathan said nothing. He was looking at Farley, smiling, as if she did not stand between them.

"Play," she said.

"Play what?"

"Oh, play," she said lightly, laughing, her voice challenging them to think of something to play. Somewhere in her being the sound of Farley's voice struck three chords of harmony. When he spoke the sky belled and the grass cymbaled, but the presence of Jonathan was a dissonance. She looked askance at him.

"Blondie," she began to chant, touching Jonathan with one extended finger, "baby blond, drowned himself in the millpond."

64

"You're the baby," Jonathan said in his equable voice, but his eyes narrowed and flashed with the heat of irritation, and he made a pass to catch her by the arm. She evaded him and began to circle the boy Farley. Jonathan tripped and clutched Farley to keep from falling. His arm remained resting on Farley's shoulder.

"You're the blond," Rhoda chanted and moved near Farley on the other side so that Jonathan would reach for her and remove his arm from about Farley. "Go drown yourself in the millpond."

Rhoda continued to chant. The elation she had felt on first seeing them enter the garden still lighted all she looked at. It touched the garden and the canna beds and absorbed the early, saturate heat of the August day, leaving her in a cell of cool joy, as if it were composed from the shade that shortened on the west side of the house. The malice with which she taunted Jonathan was touched with the same elation and it heightened the tautness of her being to see him respond, as he did now, by trying to catch her.

"Baby blond," she chanted as she caught Farley's crooked elbow and swung him around and around to keep him between herself and Jonathan. The blond boy caught Farley's other elbow and the three of them whirled and pivoted until finally they went down in a heap on the grass.

They rested then a moment. The dark boy's knee, flung out, rested, very lightly, against her thigh and carefully Rhoda did not move away. Jonathan's legs were locked about Farley's waist and suddenly the two began to struggle.

The girl watched them in silence. Her elation was held in abeyance and she was only waiting as she watched Farley shut his fingers around Jonathan's ankles, his strong, earth-colored hands dark against the flower-white of the blond boy's skin. The blood rose dark to his face in his effort to free himself from the lock of Jonathan's legs, but once he had broken free he retained his hold on the other's ankles and leaned against him, resting, until Jonathan moved apart.

For a moment there was silence and the girl Rhoda saw with a quick touch of jealousy that the gaze of the dark boy was not now for herself, but for the blond boy Jonathan who sat a little apart from them both, his thin hands immersed in a busyness with the grass.

His small bones beneath my hands, his little bones, Farley was thinking, the thought moving inscrutably behind his fine brow. He remembered how he had first approached Jonathan through aggression, the act in keeping with the June day, cool at its beginning, warming to an intemperate degree and cooling again to the mean that represented their relationship from that day forward: not cool, as at first, nor insupportable as at the climax, but a summery temperature always.

Days passed after he saw the blond boy riding his bicycle past his window before Farley saw him again. He was on his way from the library, where he had gone on an errand for his father, when he came on the blond boy resting in the shade of an elm tree. He stood, hot and sweaty, one leg thrown over the saddle of the bicycle, resting. No one else was on the street, and he approached the blond boy who had ridden by his window and waved, and stood a moment looking into his eyes. The eyes were frank and clear and seemed of the purity of spring water which has no color of its own but reflects truly the image of whatever bends above it.

"You saw me the other day," he said to the blond boy, "do you remember?"

"Yes," the other said, and stood waiting, as if he had always been waiting at one point or another for the approach of Farley.

He had considered the voice. He sensed that the soft voice was balanced on some invisible fulcrum, ready to be weighted in whatever direction would win its owner favor.

"I'll wrestle you," he said suddenly to the blond boy.

The other said nothing. He removed his leg from the seat and leaned the bicycle carefully upon its parking brace, then he moved backwards a step and stood ankle-deep in the grass under the elm, waiting.

Farley knew suddenly the feel of the slight body within his arms, even before he embraced it for the throw. He experienced a tremor of anticipation in his muscles as he approached the other. The blond boy went down beneath him so docilely he was taken aback. For a moment he wrestled with the slack body, feeling the small ribs that cased the boy's heart latticed against his palms. He released the other and sat on his body, conscious of the small hipbones hard against his own flesh, looking at him in surprise. He had meant battle. He had wanted to subdue, and the blond boy had avoided battle by a surprising stratagem, by simple surrender. He knew then that as his own defense lay in aggression the blond boy's defense was in propitiation. Still he was not ready to give it up and he delivered some half-hearted blows to the body of the boy beneath him. The eyes that looked up into his own registered neither anger nor fear. He was certain all at once that what he read in the blond boy's eyes was acceptance. His hands closed around the other's wrists, pressing until the bones beneath resisted the grip. Then he raised the blond boy without releasing him and they stood facing each other. After a moment he released his grip and his own arms fell to his side.

67

"What's your name?" he said.

"Jonathan," the other said.

"I'm Farley," he said, and smiled, and the blond boy smiled, and the beauty of his fair face under the mop of so-blond hair touched him with a sharp pain that was compounded of envy and delight and the odd feeling of regret that overtakes the pilgrim who has finally reached Mecca.

After a while they mounted the bicycle and rode away together.

All of this Farley remembered in, as it were, a glance of thought briefer than the space of time his gaze remained fixed on Jonathan's face. Jonathan, intolerable of stillness, now sprang lightly to his feet and came up to Farley and grasped his heel and began to sled him over the grass. Then he reached out with his free hand and grasped Rhoda and began to pull at them together.

"Stop!" Rhoda squealed. She felt rising even above the surface of her resumed elatedness a gladness at having something to resent. "Stop," she said as he continued to pull at them, "I hate you."

"Hate me," Jonathan said in his equable voice. He stood away from them again and looked at Farley as if to ask, what are we doing *here?* The dark boy came up to him and tripped him and they were all in a heap again, and the cats came to them, marching in single file in dignified parade to examine their antics on the grass.

"I do," Rhoda said, looking at Jonathan over the heads of the expectant and astonished cats.

"Do what?" Jonathan said.

"Hate you, hate you, hate you."

"Oh," Jonathan said, "I thought you meant you *did*."

"If I did," she said, infuriated by the casualness of his in-

68

sult, "it wouldn't be with you." And when she had said it she was angry for having been trapped. She saw at once that by her ready vulgar response she had been brought to the level he had chosen. Thinking this she stooped and picked up the cat that had wrapped itself purring around her feet.

It was Tawm.

"That's the kind of cat you need," Jonathan said.

"It's a cat. It's like any cat."

"No, it isn't."

"What kind of cat is it, then, Mister Smarty?" she said.

"It's a cut cat," Jonathan said.

"I hate you," she said. She stared at him through the morning light that was beginning to waver with heat. They were moving now along the concrete walk that ran from the kitchen porch to the summerhouse. The heat, rebounding from the concrete, wavered upward so that objects seen through it undulated in a slow dance. The great yellow male cat that had been castrated to keep him from wandering lay calmly in the girl's arms. They began to play with him, holding objects for him to bat with his paw. After a while they took a handkerchief with which he had been playing and trussed him by tying his four legs together and two of them carried him suspended from a stick in the manner of wild game. The cat made no objection beyond switching his yellow-ringed tail.

Jonathan crossed the walk and began to stroke the cat.

"He's just like Farley," he said.

"What's Farley?" the girl said. Her voice was innocent and sweet, as if she had forgotten the drift of their conversation about the cat.

"He's a cut cat," Jonathan said.

"Liar," Farley said.

69

"Do you want me to show you?" Jonathan said. They had stopped again, but now they were behind a canna bed near the summerhouse.

"I hate you," she said.

"Don't you want me to show you?" Jonathan said lightly. He caught Farley and threw him on the grass. "I'll show you."

She stood still, watching them.

"Hey!" Farley said, fighting Jonathan's hands. Then they were wrestling in the grass in an entanglement of arms and legs. Seeing their bodies in contact awoke in the girl a tension which dictated for its release a condition she did not understand.

"Stop it," she said. "I'll kill it."

"Don't," Farley said from the ground. "Don't hurt it." She had caught the great yellow cat by the throat and was slowly choking it.

"She won't," Jonathan said, "she hasn't got the nerve."

"It's you, it's not Farley," she said.

"It's Farley, it's a cut cat," Jonathan said. He lay behind Farley, holding him in a loose embrace while he stared at Rhoda, grinning.

"Stop it," Farley said.

"She won't do it," Jonathan said. "She's a sissy."

"I hate you," she said to Jonathan and continued to choke the trussed cat that struggled ineffectually in her hands.

"I say, stop it," Farley cried angrily at last.

But she couldn't stop it. Her hand had taken on a volition of its own and she watched it as if it had no connection with herself while it slowly choked the life from the great yellow cat. The cat threshed its head from side to side, struggling with a staccato sneezing sound. In a moment its red tongue ran between its teeth and the bulging eyes rolled upward. The dark boy Farley attempted to rise but Jonathan held him locked in his arms. Farley wrenched his body around and swung and hit the other a sharp blow in the face. At the moment he wrenched free the body of the cat went limp in the girl's hands and she dropped it, jerking her hands away from it as if she had held a snake.

"Oh," Farley said.

"I didn't mean to," she said.

"You did, though," he said, accusing.

"I didn't mean it," she said. "It was Jonathan's fault."

The dead cat lay between them. She felt remorse for a moment, and then she began to feel a secret pride that she had been able to strangle the cat. The cat held all her attention so that briefly she forgot the others. When she looked up again she saw that Jonathan sat on his heels slightly behind Farley. His face was red and beginning to swell from the blow. There was a solemn hurt in his eyes but even as she looked at Jonathan, Farley's hand went out in search of him and as he touched him Jonathan's face lightened under the mop of so-blond hair. Then Jonathan rose and began to walk away from them through the garden.

"She'll find the cat," Farley said. He whispered.

"I know it," Rhoda said, "and then she won't let me go to Miss Brophy's." She whispered too, making a conspiracy of it.

"We'll have to get rid of it," Farley said.

"Yes," she said, whispering above the still warm body of the dead cat.

Jonathan had come up to them again. "We'll have to bury it," he said in his husky voice, whispering too, being drawn into the conspiracy.

"Where?" the girl said, plaintive. "Where can we bury

it?" She was beginning to sob a little through the mesh of her secret pride. The fur of the dead cat stuck up between the spread fingers of her hand that rested on it like yellowed grass about sticks.

"She'd notice the grass," Farley said. "She'd notice that the first thing." He was referring to Aunt Angelicia but he did not speak her name. None of them did.

"Yes, she would," Rhoda said, whispering, "if she ever found out."

"We can bury it behind the shed," Jonathan said. "She won't notice it there." He had been scouting stealthily in the garden.

"Behind the shed?" Rhoda said, looking at Farley.

"Sure," Farley said. "Great."

"All right," she said.

They moved to the close space behind the shed, watching for Aunt Angelicia as they passed among the flower beds and the shrubs near the wall, carrying the body of the dead cat.

"What will we dig it with?" Farley said. He could not bring himself to name the hole made to receive a dead body.

"With our bare claws," Jonathan said. The other two looked at him, shocked, and then they looked at the feet of the dead cat and then at their own hands.

"There's a shovel," Rhoda said after a moment.

"Where?"

"In the shed. It's Dandelion's."

"Get it."

She got the short garden spade and they dug a small oblong in the pithy soil, moist under the shade of the maple boughs. After they had buried the cat they were a long while behind the summerhouse.

All that had been yesterday. Now she was in the garden

among the flowering cannas and if one had asked what do you bury, she could not have told, for the beast, even, as well as the events that led to its death lived as vividly in her mind as if they had not buried the cat at all.

She had been drawing near the shed, as if drawn by some force beyond her knowledge or power of control, and she was now at the south end of the summerhouse. She came close to it and looked into the narrow space between its rear wall and the wall of the garden. She stared at the small oblong that had been recently stirred in the moldy, damp soil that sweated in the shade.

When Rhoda lifted her eyes from the oblong she was staring into the eyes of Aunt Angelicia. She was not surprised, though she had not heard her aunt come to the opening at the other end of the summerhouse to stand there without shadow.

"Tawm?" Aunt Angelicia said. Her eyes were old and black and very hard.

"Yes," she said. She did not know how her aunt divined that the oblong contained the body of her favorite cat, but she found in herself no strength for denial against those hard eyes.

While she stared into the eyes of the childless woman childed by herself and the cats, as she knew, yesterday's events lived for her, vivid and wrenching. She rejected the figure of the dead cat, cast it out, and the face of Jonathan became milk-blank, without feature. Farley's face was clear and beautiful in its dark symmetry, but her dream of his face had altered. It was not accompanied by the three chords of harmony, as of music. All her dream was filled with a sodden silence, as of an invisible rain falling upon a porous soil.

Rhoda moved backwards and away from her aunt. But the woman was not seeing the girl before her. She was searching frantically for the figure in the tulle gown which for the first time did not appear at her summons.

Then the woman, too, turned away to leave the space behind the summerhouse. When they began to walk the girl and the woman were moving away from each other, and each step carried them farther and farther apart.

# XIII

THE NEGRO DANDELION stopped a moment and lifted his big hand and scythed the beaded sweat from his brow. He had just come from Miss Angeley's garden and the sight of the girl Rhoda. Once he left Miss Angeley's he continued a little way on Maple and then turned down Center Street which he followed for several blocks before turning to his right again to reach Miss Ella's house.

Before he reached Center a whinnying voice accosted him.

"Looky," the voice said.

The Negro Dandelion halted his shuffle and stared at Hester McCracken's bastard, Gin McCracken. The bastard sat like a tired frog on a sack of fertilizer that had overturned from his wheelbarrow into the gutter.

"Aah," said the Negro Dandelion.

"Youan help me?" the bastard who was called Cracker for short said. Dandelion stood for a moment before making a move to help.

"Youan help me, nigger?" Cracker said.

The Negro Dandelion stiffened. He stared speculatively at the bastard who stared back at him from violent, unlevel eyes.

75

"You ain't no nigger, are you?" Dandelion said.

"Nah," Cracker said.

"You white?"

"Just my old lady," Cracker said. He laughed with a cracked whinnying sound.

"You ain't white, though?" Dandelion said.

"Nah," Cracker said.

"If you ain't a nigger and ain't white you ain't neither."

"I'm tired," Cracker said. "Whyn you help me?"

"If you ain't neither you ain't nothin'," Dandelion persisted.

"I hast to move this here," Cracker said. He got up and lifted ineffectually at the heavy sack with his spindling arms. "Youan help me?"

"Naah," Dandelion said.

"Help me, nigger," Cracker said. "I ain't got all day."

"Naah," Dandelion said. "Get you a white man to help you." He began to shuffle forward again.

The half-black boy Cracker began to curse the other. He spewed obscenities at him in a high whinnying voice.

The Negro Dandelion stopped again and stared back at Cracker with a half-threatening gaze.

"You ain't neither, you ain't nothin'," Dandelion said. The two, both maimed, stood a moment in immortal light and stared meanly at each other. After a little Cracker sat down on the sack again, ignoring Dandelion, and began beating time to some inner rhythm or music which only he knew.

If she had let me have a quarter, Dandelion thought, his mind returning to Miss Angeley as he made his way down the street. He was filled with a mixed resentment against Miss Angeley and the half-caste Cracker as he turned onto Center Street to go to Miss Ella's house. Miss Ella lived on a cross street that connected Center Street with the fringe of the town where the Negro himself lived.

I'll be there, Dandelion thought, I'll be there in a minute. And he began to think of something besides Miss Angeley and Cracker. He began to think of a dip of snuff.

# XIV

IT WAS still the morning of the day of the Negro Dandelion's death, and the blond boy Jonathan was on his way to Farley's house. *When I see the blood,* the blond boy thought, and in his mind the words issued from the mouth of the Reverend Mr. Carhorn, who was pastor of the First Church of Tilden. He had heard Mr. Carhorn on the Sunday preceding and by now the vision of him was a little dim and merged somewhat with Egyptian night and the imperfectly perceived angel of dark portent passing, pausing, hovering, testing whom to strike.

Lintel without blood, thought the blond boy, associating himself vaguely with an imperfect image—he was not sure what a lintel was—for under the spell of Reverend Carhorn he had felt that the dark angel could not possibly spare him as he listened. Then from the preaching memory came the second phrase of the text, *I will pass over thee,* and the boy was taken with fascination by the image of the pastor's mobile mouth. It seemed to issue words as if each were unwrapped in a separate action from the full lips. There was, too, something about it that reminded him of the mouth of a fish lipping food under water so he was sometimes startled

to hear audible speech coming from the Reverend Mr. Carhorn unimpeded by lap or depth.

The sun was over the hills now. It was near nine o'clock,
and the heat and light of the August day dispelled the Egyptian dark from the Reverend Mr. Carhorn's text as remembered by the blond boy, but the words remained and his
mind played with them still as he moved with his light stride
along the street. When I see the blood eye, he thought.

Jonathan lived with his parents and five brothers on the
east side of Tilden and to reach his friend Farley's house he
had to go all the way across town. He usually traversed the
distance on his bicycle which had belonged to his brothers
before him and had been handed down one to the other as
each grew toward manhood until now it was Jonathan's alone
and his to keep. He was the youngest son and, as it were,
without heir. It never occurred to him that his elder brothers
had been scrupulous in keeping the bicycle in good repair,
prolonging it in service to an incredible age through a mechanical proficiency inherited from their father who was a
loom service man in Clifton Mills. Yet, as it had been given
him in good condition, he gave it meticulous care and kept
it shining with paint and polish and the spokes and sprockets
taut and tight. When he rode the bicycle, light flew from
the turning wheels in spangles and shot from the handle bars
and mudguards as they caught the sun.

On this day the blond boy was without his mount. He had
broken a spoke in the rear wheel and his third brother had
promised to buy one for him at the service shop on his way
from work that afternoon.

"That will please you, huh?" his third brother said.

"Sure it will," Jonathan said. "Thanks."

"What will you do today without the wheel?"

"I'll go to Farley's," Jonathan said. He looked at his brother from the innocent blue depth of eyes in which there was never any revelation.

"Don't you always?" his brother said, and then added, "What do you two do together all the time?"

"We play with each other," Jonathan said.

"I'll bet you do," the third brother said. The blond boy still looked at his brother from the depth of innocence and though there was no rebuke in his gaze, the third brother of Jonathan felt rebuked for the insinuation he had made. "I'll remember the spoke," he said in a different tone and left abruptly for his work.

The blond boy passed through the morning town. He moved with a light stride along the street. Soon he was on the square of the town sparsely sprinkled with shoppers and farmers and their families from the countryside. These were the people he always saw on the streets, and he carried himself among them observant but remote and filled with the particularity of himself. When I see the blood, thought the blond boy, looking into store windows or meeting the gaze of bearded farmers with his equable bland stare. People always looked at the blond boy a little longer than at others, and sometimes the looker turned about or turned his head and followed him with his eyes. Jonathan was aware of this; it was a phenomenon that had its own validity but touched him no more than if he were not its cause. He was himself. People could look at him or not and the total that was himself remained the same sum.

When I see thee, blood, the blond boy said to himself. At the bank the head teller was just opening the doors for business. A little knot of people straggled on the sidewalk before the bank in the awkward attitudes of countrymen who pretend not to be waiting while they wait. The bank was the only business in town that opened as late as nine o'clock. The lateness of the opening hour was a matter for a little resentment among the countrymen, for otherwise Tilden was a soon town. The other business establishments opened promptly at eight o'clock if not earlier. If one came to shop it was irksome to wait an additional hour before being able to get a check cashed or to ask about a loan. Even if one wanted to deposit money the bank's hours were the same. Still, it was everywhere recognized that the bank's right to its implacable regimen was determined by the value of its commodity.

I will pass over thee, thought the blond boy as he left the bank with its small crowd behind. A little farther on he met the banker Mr. Darlington himself tacking his tremendous bulk up the street. He was sweating profusely under his strict straw Panama.

"Ah, good morning," Mr. Darlington said to the boy.

"Good morning, sir," Jonathan said. He turned a little to watch how Mr. Darlington advanced himself along the street with his tacking fat man's stride.

And then he forgot Mr. Darlington. He was before the First Church of Tilden and he looked up to the windows and saw the figures of Christ and the lilies and the lambs, all dead without light; and inside he saw the image of the Reverend Mr. Carhorn in his terrible yet gentle exhortative stance, and his long, heavy, gesturing hands. Then he remembered the whole text that had been in his mind all morning: *And the blood shall be to you for a token upon the houses where ye are: and when I see the blood I will pass over you, and the plague shall not be upon you to destroy you, when I smite the land of Egypt.*

81

Token, blood and plague, thought the blond boy. The phrase had a great weight in his mind but he did not understand it. He stopped walking and stood a moment before the exact center of the closed door of the church to see how it would strike him. No one was about the church, though he knew the Reverend Mr. Carhorn wrote or dozed in his study behind the sanctuary. He waited. But nothing struck him. He caught no feeling of life from the placed stones of the church as he did from the polished marble of the bank's façade, and he left it behind him, glancing back once to behold it silent, massive and heavily shadowed westward.

Maple Street rose gently from the town square. When he had gone a few blocks along it he could see the whole square a little below him. It was the same as he had seen it time and time again; still, almost, sunk in a depth of light through which the people visible to him moved as under water over their heads. He knew that the sparsity of the people visible to him was deceptive. The greater number were housed and invisible, and the fact gave the town an aura of secrecy. It was as if the people were hiding, awaiting a moment of disaster or catastrophe to disgorge from the doors in a pour of activity. When I see the blood, thought the blond boy. Once he touched a doorpost and brought his hand away untinctured. It was absent upon the posts of all the doors.

Now that the square of the town was behind him, Jonathan stopped thinking about it and his mind moved on ahead of him to Farley's house. When he thought of the dark boy he hurried a little.

"Looky," a voice said suddenly at his shoulder. He felt the quick brush of a hand.

The blond boy turned and faced the speaker.

"Oh," he said, "it's you."

"Yeah," the half-caste Gin McCracken said, looking around as if to see who else. "Youan help me?" Cracker was a little older than the blond boy but a head shorter. He looked at the blond boy with eyes that stared violently out of his purplish-black face.

"Help you what?" Jonathan said.

"Looky," Cracker said. He pointed to an overturned wheelbarrow in the gutter and a sack of fertilizer that had rolled from it.

The blond boy looked at the overturned load.

"Youan help me?" Cracker said. "I been here a hour." There was a weight of impatience in his whinnying voice.

"Sure," Jonathan said, "let's heave."

"Youan help me, then," Cracker said. With the blond boy he lifted at the heavy sack of fertilizer with his spindling arms and the veins stood out in the flesh streaked strawberry color. In a moment they had the wheelbarrow and its load righted and on the sidewalk again.

"Now," Cracker said, "that othern wouldn't do it."

"Who?" Jonathan said.

"That othern," Cracker said. He grasped the handles of the wheelbarrow and pulled by the too heavy load went staggering bent half double down the street.

The blond boy stared after Cracker as he made his way down the street. That othern, Jonathan repeated to himself. He knew whom Cracker meant. It struck him as odd that he felt himself beyond the reach of the comparative in relation to the half-caste. For a moment Jonathan remained still. Then he began to walk again in the same direction Cracker was going. The smell of fertilizer was rich on his hands and it reminded him of the odor of earth in the space between the walls behind Angelicia's summerhouse. That space, in

83

his thought, was populated by himself, Farley, the girl and the body of the dead cat. When I see the blood, thought Jonathan. There had been none, even at the death of the cat. He touched the bruise on his face where the dark boy had struck him. It was a little painful. His fingers caressed the bruise and he thought of the dark boy, and then he walked hurriedly, giving his thoughts only to the immediates of the street.

When he reached Farley's house Jonathan learned that the dark boy was not there, and he left again, moving with his light stride through the morning town. When I see the blood, he thought. He returned home by a way different from the one he had come, by bystreets, and after a little while he came near Miss Ella's house and saw the Negro Dandelion enter.

I will pass over thee, thought the blond boy and he waited awhile in the shadow of an elm and the smoke rose soon from the flue of Miss Ella's house, rising straight and blue into the concave morning.

When I, the blond boy thought, and began to walk again, skirting lightly along the street. See the blood, he thought, and his mind went for a moment to the misshapen figure of the Negro. Soon he forgot him. He was out of sight of Miss Ella's house. He passed the Brophys' and from inside came a harmony of Bach's, the treble answered by the bass and all of it coming in a swell out of the house triumphant as if on wings.

# XV

By eight o'clock on that morning of August 19th, Miss Ella lay in the rigors of madness. She could not tell what time it was though she thought once in a moment of lucidity that it was morning, for the quality of light when all was not darkness was like that of the sun and not like that of an electric lamp. She did not know how long she had lain in bed with the light coming and going, as if her house moved past trees or other objects that blotted out the sun now and then. Time meant nothing to Miss Ella because she could not extricate the present from the past. Her mind had lost grip on the moment as a point of reference and therefore was unable to calibrate time. She had memory, but it was without order, and frightening. It was true that in the rushing torrent of mental images that poured through her mind now and then there emerged, serene and gold with the sun, a figment of memory that was of yesterday morning. The thing that proved Miss Ella mad was the fact that she did not know where the fragment of memory belonged in its relation to the present and in relation to all other memory. If she had been able to establish even one moment of memory definitely she could have ordered all others by it and come to sanity, at least temporarily.

She no more knew she was mad, however, than she knew how to account for the presence of the lambs. At first there was only one. It cried at intervals. She had always loved lambs but she could not bear to hear them cry. Nothing was sadder to her than the cry of a lamb. In autumn when the wind had blown with a touch of frost through the upland pastures of her father's farm the lambs had cried and she felt all the cold of approaching winter burying in her bones. That was when she was a young woman. A very young woman, when she was growing up.

When the lamb cried she was again a child and her memories from childhood were lucid and lovely with order. But the moments of order never lasted very long, even when established by the crying of the lamb. They disrupted into darkness. Then the serene leaf that was of yesterday morning turned in a slow waltz with shadow and wind and became a tree flowered with a million wallpaper prints.

When this faded she was in a house whose windows opened on perilous seas in faery lands forlorn. With Shelley's drowned breath she was in the jumbled shouting seas. The waves bore her swiftly forward and then were reversed and bore her past shores that reminded her of Becket Foster's drawings of coasts abrupt by English seas.

On emerging from the darkness of the waves she saw the second thing that kept recurring in her mind with the sharp clarity of a scene washed in October sunlight: A landscape she had known in her childhood, and two figures walking through that landscape.

The arsonist of her imagination edged all things with fire, so that the man and woman her mind summoned upon the lane that ran through the country of her growing up wore a nimbus of red light, as if they burned with cool, translucent flame upon the road.

Sometimes it occurred to her briefly that she was in her house on the extreme edge of Tilden. She knew then that she was alone and helpless. When this happened she stared wide-eyed at the ceiling and felt a pressure at her heart as if it were being squeezed by a giant hand. At these moments her sight failed also, coming and going with the waves of pressure at her heart. If her mind had been itself this would have struck her as the physical manifestation of nostalgia, but when the light broke, splintering against darkness, she knew only terror and she wanted to scream but it seemed to her that, as in a nightmare, she could not make a sound.

The creatures of fire moved along the road. With the appearance of the figures the second lamb came also and now there were two and they cried from some hidden spot. As for the figures, they were always passing, never gone. In the scene, which must have had some particular significance if she had been able to discover it, the two figures approached a certain point in the landscape, and then she was distracted and when she was able to turn her attention to the couple again they were still approaching the same point, as if they trod a treadmill.

Once the two figures disappeared and in their place a huge black head loomed, though the head approached from the other direction, coming toward her rather than moving away as the fire figures did. The head was frightening, being without torso or legs, but on the face was a look of compassion so that she was not afraid of it. It seemed the great head spoke and smiled, even called her name, but then the face was displaced by darkness and she could not see the face; and with the feeling of helplessness and aloneness that shut about her she screamed, and this time she heard the sound ringing brassily in her ears. The next instant she saw the head again, now moving away. She could see only the back of the head. It was covered with a close mat of black hair and it

87

jerked in her vision, as if its means of locomotion were injured, as if it went lame.

There came a time, though she had no idea when it was, that as the fire figures reached a point, the sector of the landscape they never passed, she was there to confront them. The male figure faced her, and she knew him, reading the familiar lineaments of his face formed in fire. The face of the male burned in longing, but the face of the other figure was turned away so that she did not recognize it, only the halo of burning hair was shaped about a head somewhat like her own. She gave her attention to the face she knew, then, and the look of longing that it wore called up in her a terrible affirmation.

Then the voice of the person by his side, or her own voice, or that of an intruder from yesterday or the house next door was asking and asking. She saw the burning face before her and because of the urge to affirm, she said loudly: Yes, yes, yes.

Then the voices, her own and that of the questioner, were drowned by the crying of the lambs.

# XVI

AMONG his patrons the Negro Dandelion numbered Miss Ella. He did the chores about her house, and when she did not go early to the bookstore and wished to lie in bed as long as possible she arranged to have Dandelion come and build her morning fire. When he had built the fire and fed it until the oven was hot he would go and stand just inside her door with his hat in his hand and call softly if she were asleep: "Miss Ella, Miss Ella."

When she replied sleepily and petulantly, "Yes, Dandy," he shuffled out of her room and through the kitchen door, where he picked up the garbage pail to carry to his own house to be emptied among the scrawny chickens he kept in a wire pen back of his shanty.

On this August morning Dandelion built Miss Ella's fire as usual. He was casting about in his mind as to how he might ask her for a quarter, but when he entered her room and saw her lying tousled among her disordered covers he sensed that something was wrong.

"Miss Ella?" Dandelion said.

Miss Ella stared at him with wide, troubled eyes, and he saw that she did not recognize him.

"Miss Ella, you sick?" he said. He spoke in a soft, caressing tone such as he might use with a child. He was fond of Miss Ella.

She did not answer and he saw that she did not see him, though her wide staring eyes were looking directly into his own. He came a little nearer her bed, shuffling, and bent and peered into Miss Ella's eyes. At that moment they reflected a great hunger, a hunger Dandelion did not understand.

"Miss Ella hungry?" the Negro Dandelion asked. He meant for food. He could have understood the hunger which was really Miss Ella's only without relating it to its source. There were many times when he lay in his ill-smelling bed hungry beyond words, but with a hunger no food could satisfy. He too was alone in the world, but because Miss Ella was white he assumed it made a difference, that she, being white and privileged, could somehow appease all her hungers.

He had no answer from Miss Ella. He stood looking down at her and then he spoke to her, "Miss Ella sick," he said. "I'll go get somebody to come and see about Miss Ella." He bowed slightly toward her and then he began to shuffle toward the door. In his slow progress, hindered by his attempt to hurry, he glanced over his shoulder and saw that her eyes were clouded and anguished.

Suddenly she screamed.

He was transfixed by the sound of her screaming, and then he began to run in wavering grotesque strides because of his lameness. His panic was subconscious. He had not to reason what inference a hearer would draw from the scream of a white woman in the presence of a Negro. He began to pray without forming the words that no one would see him leaving Miss Ella's house. He prayed with every fiber of his body, with his whole hope of life he prayed as his shambling bones carried him uncertainly up the street.

As he ran he glanced at the house nearest Miss Ella's and saw that the iron-jawed woman who did the cleaning there was standing on the back stoop with a broom in her hand. She was looking directly at him, her broom poised. Suddenly she shouted to him.

"Nigger, what you do to that white woman?"

He gave all his energy to increasing his speed but his misshapen legs would carry him no faster.

"Come back here, you black nigger," the woman shouted, shaking her broom at him. Then she flung the broom from her and began to run in the direction of Miss Ella's house. He tasted then a green brassiness in his saliva and his body went slack for a split second so that his knees became entangled and threw him. When he rose he yearned harder than ever toward his own house, so that a part of his mind got there ahead of his body and was watching and saw him crumble at the edge of the yard against a chicken coop that stood among some trees a hundred feet or so from the house.

He collapsed before the coop and lay panting for a while. Then he pulled himself to a sitting position, managing his useless legs with his hands, and eased his back against the coop. He sat there flat on the ground, his legs straight out before him. They were as useless as two crooked sticks.

After a while the sun crept to his feet and then up his legs and finally bathed him entirely in light.

Meanwhile the iron-jawed woman from the house next door hurried into Miss Ella's house, and when she saw her lying senseless among the disheveled covers she was sure that her dreadful hope had been realized. But because she needed corroboration she began to question Miss Ella. She questioned her with the nagging persistency of a child begging for withheld sweets.

"Yes, yes, yes," Miss Ella said. But she spoke to the figure with the face of fire that moved in her fantasy.

Because of the odd, longing quality of her voice the cleaning woman looked at her, startled, a moment before she hurried from that house to spread the news of the violation of Miss Ella. It did not occur to her that though Miss Ella needed medical attention it was not for the suturing of a virgin violated.

Or perhaps it did and she was disinclined toward the truth.

"I always said if that nigger," she said aloud, and her eyes darted about her, secret and hostile, as if she were watching him from a dirty window, he shuffling with his eyes averted from her, shuffling slowly up the street of no name.

# XVII

In the Brophys' parlor a pupil practiced an air of Bach's, a little two-part invention that stated a theme of pure joy and then repeated itself like a marvelous bird enchanted by its own song. The cleaning woman could hear it from Miss Ella's house, and it was audible still when she reached the house below and there told her news to the first person she encountered, the White's washerwoman caught midway between the back door and the washpot with a load of dirty laundry in her arms.

Once she had begun the rumor it was as if the woman disappeared. In their concern with the word itself no one remembered the teller. So it was that no one knew definitely how it began, only that its source was a house on the back streets of Tilden with a single woman occupant, a woman the whole town knew, for everyone knew everyone else in Tilden. If Miss Ella had been a stranger it might have turned out differently. The rumor might have been absorbed into the vacuity of a lack of information. It might have fallen inert somewhere between the demands of the double question, who? what?

There were no such demands and the rumor prospered. It was like a seed planted in season and well watered, though for all anyone could certainly say it might have been the wind's affair. At this time of the year there was always a wind stirring in the streets. It was the warm, leaf-fetid breath of August and it disturbed all it touched. At night, when it did not lessen, the dogs of the town stirred restlessly and howled, their voices carrying far into the country beyond, so that farmyard dogs answered in kind, keeping people from their sleep. Dawns broke with an unhealthy warmth in the air, as if by daybreak the sun were already two hours high, and the people who met on the streets of Tilden in the early morning nodded listlessly to each other, and passed. They felt already drained and depleted. It was a perfect weather for catastrophe.

Soon the incident was vouched and known and no longer the wind's affair. Rumor became fact, was of witness and corroborated. Here and there it was denied and laughed down, but the denial met with no belief. Eagerly testimony was cited, for the violence of the August days that knit into great clouds and thundered over Tilden gathered again in the people's blood. They remembered dogs howling in the night and their skins prickled and their nerves shivered in an ecstasy of promise and threat which grew as the rumor spread, its fragments gathering to a single mass:

"I hear she saw him out by the back."

"What was he doing?"

"Moving away from the house. Running."

"Who's *she?* The one he . . . ?"

"Not her . . ."

"The woman who works for the lady that lives next door. What's her name? She told the Whites' washerwoman who . . ."

"It was Hamby told it."

94

"Stark . . ."

"Seabolt . . ."

"It was . . ."

"But who *saw* it?"

"As I say, it was . . ."

"But did she *say* he did it herself?"

"Not that I heard . . ."

"No."

"Yes."

"Dandelion wouldn't do it."

"I've known Dandy all his life. Why he's like a . . ."

"He works for her don't he?"

"Dandelion wouldn't do a thing like that."

"God damn his rusty hide."

"It's all a lie, every bit of it. You'll see . . ."

"We'll stretch his black neck."

"You'll see he didn't . . ."

"We'll see, all right. By God, we'll make him tell!"

As the single leaves one sees blown in opposite directions come often to rest in the same drift, for the wind both disperses and gathers, by devious passes the scraps of speech, of charge and accusation, that had their beginnings on the back streets of Tilden, cohered and the clear tale they told was that the Negro Dandelion had raped Miss Ella, the thin, ageless spinster who kept a bookstore on the square of the town, and left her raving and senseless on her bed.

This news, for it was no longer a rumor, with a will and strength of its own and almost as if it had a tangible presence, traveled from the side streets of Tilden inward toward the center of the town. Somehow it came to the blacksmith shop and when it was spoken to him the great smith, dark from the soot of the forge, stood a moment and stared at the plow glowing hot from the furnace which he held outward from him in the jaws of the tongs. Then he looked at the farmer Abraham who had brought the plow to be sharpened. They nodded to each other and the smith made a short jabbing movement as if he meant to brand the air with the glowing iron, then flung the plow from him and the tongs after it. These landed in a heap of scrap iron with a great clatter and their clanging reverberations followed the two through the door as they came out upon the street.

By other agents it reached the periphery of the square composed largely of stores and shops. After it was known there the people avoided looking at each other, caught in a strange tide of inwardness or of embarrassment or, perhaps, dread. In the stores the usually courteous clerks grew impatient and drummed on the counters with their knuckles while waiting for the customers to find change, for it had come to the clerks too. Their bodies seemed to lengthen and strain forward from their waists toward the open doorways like strange plants growing toward light. The customers themselves snapped at the clerks more than usual and when they had made their purchases hurried out on the streets again.

At last it reached the square itself. The loiterers, lethargic and sleepy, the shopping farmers idling in the lull of late summer, and all that were on the square soon sensed the matter that was abroad and were electrified into a brief kinetic frenzy. Only two men kept throughout a serene calm. From his desk in the rear of the bank Mr. Darlington kept his eyes fastened upon the door. He knew by the slackness of business that something was not as usual in Tilden. Yet he was confident that if anything were amiss he would be consulted in its righting, and he sat in that confidence, willing to wait.

The tellers at the windows had no such assurance; they shifted from foot to foot, drawn toward the street, but the stare of Mr. Darlington kept them fixed at their posts. In his study behind the First Church of Tilden the Reverend Mr. Carhorn drowsed and nodded over his next Sunday's sermon, half prepared. He heard nothing but now and then the intermittent buzz of a fly trapped between his window glass and the wire of the screen, and once the sound of passing footsteps that seemed to stalk a quarry, as in his half-thoughts and half-dreams he pursued the subject of his sermon with a stealth of mind.

About that time the hunter Nimrod Anse, with the smell of hounds and the woods still on him, walked with his tireless gait past the church and on toward Mr. Darlington's bank. To him, fresh from the woods, the town wore a strange atmosphere. He walked more than a block puzzling the matter. It was not until he passed the milliner's shop and saw the woman peering with her avid gaze around the inner door through the closed shop that he knew why the town seemed unusually strange: Nowhere was there a woman on the streets. The woman he saw in the shop withdrew her head, quickly, on catching his glance but once he was past stood farther into the door where she could better see; nothing escaped the alert eye of the hunter.

When the hunter arrived at the mailbox before Mr. Darlington's bank he stopped and leaned against it, resting his thin shanks firmly against the metal. He stood aloof, as if in the middle of woods or fields, and observed the crowd.

For a while the men were only eager informants or equally avid listeners. They drew into swiftly formed groups and clusters that as quickly dissolved, the separate members moving apart to draw about themselves, through the mag-

97

netism of their secretive looks or knowing airs, others not yet informed.

There came a time, a particular moment, when the whole shape of things changed. Something drew the scattered groups momentarily into a single body. It emptied the buildings. For a little no one remained in the stores and shops, even to guard the tills. All were caught in the common concern. They built to a mass that jelled in the glare of nearing noon and was for a little while without movement. Then the mass suddenly broke and dispersed. That was the moment the men of Tilden, on the converged-upon square, accepted the rumor as truth and joined their wills in a single determination. Without apparent communication their intent was transmitted one to another and validated by unanimous acceptance.

They intended to lynch the Negro Dandelion.

The wind that blew in Tilden that day only shook the windows gently or moved the paper debris scudding along the sidewalks a little way, but the men moved outward from the square as if driven by a gale of irresistible force. They did not all continue at once in the same direction but parted and went separate ways. Their movements seemed undeliberated, aimless. But their purpose was clear in their own minds. It was only that they could approach the execution of their will more speedily and with less chance of interference by indirection. Finally, with the exception of Anse the hunter who preferred the blood of the fox, the men were all going in the direction of Clifton Mills.

For a moment after the men were gone there was a perfect silence on the square. Across town at the Brophys', the house next to Miss Ella's where it all began, the forgotten pupil still practiced the air by Bach. The character of the music had changed, had become infused with torpor or melancholy. But it was not cognizant. It was only that the pupil, too long forgotten by Miss Brophy, was tiring and her hands dragged a little on the keys.

# XVIII

ALL the morning the boy Farley had been on the streets pursuing his pleasure. The pursuit led him through the town and back again. It was an arduous campaign because of the elusiveness of his quarry. The promise of early success which he glimpsed in the most unlikely places, in drugstore booths, in the dark dirty alleys between the buildings on the town square, suffered postponement. These places proved not the cul-de-sacs he thought them. A way opened, sometimes as mysteriously as the Red Sea's dividing, and the quarry escaped.

At first he was not conscious of anything unusual about the morning town. He passed in concentration by groups of men gathered in knots on the street, unaware. Finally their silence, when he was in earshot, penetrated his consciousness. He began to be furtive and subtle, pretending disinterest, and by much stealth managed to overhear a phrase, now from this group, now from that. He kept in his mind each crumb of speech stolen ant-like from beneath the stony, watchful stares of the men. These he fitted together like the pieces of a jigsaw puzzle, and after a while he had the story.

When he had filched a complete knowledge from the men his first impulse was to laugh. When a boy of his own age recounted to a group an exploit like the one which according to the men the Negro Dandelion accomplished the others laughed as if it were the funniest thing in the world. They did not laugh in true amusement but to hide their embarrassment and outraged innocence, and to deny the importance attached to a matter that had their constant concern. What is important that you can laugh at? But Farley was alone and had no need of any shift. He went silently along the streets, the serious intonations of speech blowing about him like a dark weather. If it had been before yesterday he would have had no conception of what had been penetrated or profaned, but the interval behind the summerhouse had prepared him; and now it involved him in menace which he felt only as a fitful chill under his skin.

With the thing he had heard about her, Miss Ella took on a new importance in his mind, and it occurred to him suddenly to go to her house and see for himself. For if such a serious offense as the voices of the men implied had been committed against Miss Ella it must leave its visible sign. If he could see her he would know if the thing the men told of were true.

He set out for Miss Ella's house at a brisk walk. He had visited her often before, bringing her cakes from his mother's oven, or a new recipe his mother wanted Miss Ella to try; or simply visiting to half-listen to her gay, bird-like chatter while he pored over the books from her bulging cases on the carpeted floor.

Miss Ella's was the last house on the street. Beyond her house the street became a highway and soon vanished from sight into the world of woods and fields that bordered the town of Tilden. Beyond the house he could see the green fields of August, limp emerald in the growing heat of the day. Somewhere near, he knew, was the house of the Negro Dandelion, and he wondered now what the Negro was doing, what he felt after having been with Miss Ella. It seemed to him that Dandelion must be a changed man for no one, he thought, could experience that and be the same. Though he was now initiate, it was still much a ritual of mystery that held his mind and activated his glands deep in the secrets of his flesh.

Before Miss Ella's house he felt momentarily a reluctance to enter but there was no difficulty attendant to abet his impulse to retrace his steps. The door stood open and he knocked lightly and entered before anyone could respond to his knocking. The living room was empty. His eyes went to the familiar bookcases and nothing was changed there. Titles he remembered were in their remembered places. The living room was neat in the mode of Miss Ella's neatness, orderly in disarray.

A sweet disorder in the dress, Miss Ella was fond of quoting, and he thought of the words and still had them in his mind when a large, rawboned woman he had never seen entered.

"Well, bless my soul," the woman said, "who are you?"

"I'm Farley," he said. "I came to see Miss Ella."

"Now ain't that sweet of you," the woman said. He could not tell whether she meant the words or was mocking him.

"May I see her?" he said.

The woman ignored his question. She stooped a little toward him. "Do you know what happened to her?" she asked in a loud whisper. "Do you?"

"Yes," he said.

The woman straightened as if he had slapped her and looked at him sternly. "Who told you," she said, "a tyke like you?"

"Nobody," he said, "I just heard."

"I bet you did," she said.

"May I see her?" he said again, not looking at the iron-jawed woman, for as he compared her with his mother and Miss Ella she offended him. He resented her whole presence in the same way an art lover resents an inferior work of art.

"No indeed," the woman said. "Now why do you want to see her?" And she added in an intimate tone, "Because of *that?*"

He was shocked, first because the woman had read his mind, and next because the thing she had discerned was in his mind to read.

"Ah, no," he objected, "not because of that."

"Why, then?" the woman said.

"I always come to see her," he said. "Can I see her now?"

"No," the woman said, "you can't see her now . You don't want to see her. She's crazy."

"Crazy!" Farley said.

"Crazy as a loon," the woman said. "After what happened to her. Now get on with you. She will be wanting someone with her." The woman stood cradling an elbow in each hand waiting for him to leave. He made no move to go and finally the woman's eyes shifted from him, veering away in indifference. "I've got to go now," she said. She turned to re-enter Miss Ella's room.

He followed her to the bedroom door. He could see Miss Ella lying thin and tense among the covers the iron-jawed cleaning woman had made straight and neat.

While he looked at Miss Ella his mind moved backward

and he remembered her on a former visit sitting in her chair in the living room where he now stood, saying in her high, light voice:

"I had a sweetheart once myself."

She had looked at him and because of something in his face or to convince herself she added, "Really I did."

He remembered what he had thought then as she looked at him with her head held delicately to one side. She looks like a bird, he had thought, just like a bird.

"Who was he?" he had said, then, and despite his upbringing in the virtues of politeness he could not make his voice firm with interest. It had a falseness of timbre he could not disguise.

"Oh, he was just a man," Miss Ella said, failing to admit the falseness of his show of interest, her voice running over it to drown it. "You wouldn't know who it was if I told you. You see, you never saw him. Besides, it was a long time ago and it was in another country." Time flowed a little between them before she added, "Did you ever read *The Jew of Malta?*"

"No," he had said, "why?"

"*The Jew of Malta* is by Christopher Marlowe. You've read Christopher Marlowe in school. I'm sure you have."

" 'Was this the face that launched a thousand ships?' " Farley began because the line had stuck in his mind. He had misread it. He had missed the sense and confused the face with the ways of a shipyard.

But Miss Ella interrupted him with a way she had of making a pouting small face when she became impatient.

"That's not from *The Jew of Malta*," she said. "Of course it isn't."

"But what has what you were saying got to do with your

sweetheart?" Farley said, and his interest in this point was genuine and his voice firm and eager.

"Oh, there is a line in *The Jew of Malta* which reads like this, 'But that was in another country.' " Miss Ella paused a moment, taking the inside of her lips between her teeth in embarrassment as she remembered what it was that was lost in that other country. "You see," she went on, "I was quoting Marlowe without intending to. It goes to show how one's reading will affect one. But I wasn't talking about *The Jew of Malta*. I meant that when I was young I didn't live here. I lived in another part of the country. I've told you where I was reared, I'm sure I have. Anyway, it was there I had this sweetheart."

Then Miss Ella had become silent. In her memory she passed backward through time until she was seventeen again in the high house of her father, at the dip of the country between the mountains and the sea. The boy Farley with his young dark face was transformed in her vision and she saw again the young man who had been in love with her in that land that lay calm between the undulations of mountains and sea. Diffident he stood, with his hat in his hands, turning it, his doubtful smile crooking his mouth, she never saw him smile without knowing a sudden desire to kiss him; and she stood at the door to greet him, holding it wide and saying, "Come in, do come in!" and hearing as if it had been only yesterday his doubtful, "Ah, perhaps . . ." He was two years her elder, older than she, and she often thought (she did often think) that the disparity in their ages, small as it was, had been fatal to their love. She loved him, too. Of course she did. He was a strong young man with the awkward graces, the appealing graces, of the countryman put upon his mettle by his peers. He had no betters, and recognized none. Yet he was diffident as he stood at her door, for her father was well-to-do in that country and he, her lover, had nothing but the strength of his body and title to three hundred acres of land lying rich but neglected and run-down near the porch of the sea.

Yet it was not his poverty, he was not really poor, being propertied, but without money, that had come between them. No, it was the difference in their ages that had been their undoing. He with his need (he often said) in his breast a thing he could not restrain without damage to himself. He often said it, flashing his hurt and crooked smile. And she was a foolish dove. A pure silly. She had a notion that she wanted learning. She was to go to finishing school, for her father would send her. "Wait," she had often told him in that sacred summer, "two years is a short time (it will make our love grow stronger) and I will come back to you. And I will dream of you every day I am away. I swear it."

She had dreamed of him for thirty years.

He had not liked the idea of waiting. No, he had not liked the idea of her going away to school. "Marry me, marry me now," he had said, and she remembered the road they had taken on their last walk together in that summer of fire. It was a service road that led nowhere except between her father's fields to a dead end of woods dark to the west. "No," she had said, touching him lightly. "No, you must wait for me. It will prove that you love me." (A silly girl to be set-ting a man a love-trial and he no knight nor of the age of knighthood.) "I won't wait for you," he had said. "Listen to me," he said. "Marry me now. I won't wait for you."

It had been the difference in their ages. She had simply not needed him enough. Not then. She had kissed his bitter mouth lightly and answered him nothing.

They had been very near to the woods.

What was it? Surely she had had no such love of knowl-edge as to barter love for learning. What quaint notions girls had then in the peach-blossom time of Girlhood. She had gone away to school. Lightly she had gone, for she had not believed him when he swore he would not wait for her. She went away for the term and he did not write to her, and when she returned he was gone. Strangers were upon his lands. He had taken his doubtful eyes and crooked smile away from her. He carried somewhere else his need.

She heard he had gone to sea. (Wide waters claiming his history known no further upon the land, a man rejected by his lover, self-exiled, wifeless, to the impressionless waters of the sterile sea.)

What, then, could a cultivated young lady of question-able beauty do but what she had done? With the legacy from her father she set herself up in the genteel business of selling books (O heroes and heroines of paper) to the genteel peo-ple of the town of Tilden.

She had prospered moderately.

All of this she did not convey to the boy Farley but with-out being able to tell what she was thinking he had sensed something of the mood and matter of her reverie on that earlier visit, and now Miss Ella lay on her bed and turned her head fretfully from side to side while the August heat squeezed from that dry rind of a woman a few globules of sweat that rolled like bubbles of mercury from her parched forehead. There was no distinct sign of what had happened to her visible to Farley, no sign at all.

When he thought of this he grew perfectly still. He stared at Miss Ella without seeing her. The edges of his mind were in agitation from the movement of submerged thought. He

did not know at once what concept moved there, then suddenly, like a clear shape from a pool's depth, the thought
emerged with perfect clarity in his mind. He still gave the
thought no words but now he possessed a new knowledge.
It doesn't show, he thought, thinking of the thing that had
been committed against Miss Ella.

Mysteriously and without volition his mind went then to
Jonathan, by-passing by some secret way not known or
marked by the boy its more immediate concern with the
girl Rhoda. He knew a sudden sense of elation, as if he had
won an unexpected lap in an unforeseen, forced race.

He broke from his stance of stillness with a spontaneous
dance step. No sign, his mind said, no mark. The unseeing
eyes of Miss Ella turned toward him and fixed him in a
feverish stare. Recalled to the room, he watched for a
moment, the knowledge that Miss Ella was crazy sharp at
the small of his back, like the point of a knife. Then he
looked at the rough-featured woman who had taken up her
position in a chair facing Miss Ella. The woman turned her
head and looked at him in the doorway with perfect indifference. She began a soft croon that had in it the drowse of
sleep. She sat, nursing each elbow in a big, red hand and soon
she began to rock back and forth in her bedside vigil.

"Crazy."

He said the word to himself. Soon he was out of the house
and on the street. The chemistry of his body was changed
and the tides that had hurried his blood receded. He was
again his normal self in the circle of usual day, but he kept
within easy thought-reach his new, secret knowledge. He
called it forth now and then to startle the familiars of his
mind, and it was much as if a wandering bear breached the
edge of a thicket to stare upon a pasture of docile sheep.

# XIX

THE BOY Farley had walked among the men without being aware at first of all that was in their minds. He had heard the news of the rape of Miss Ella and it moved him in a way he did not wholly understand, causing him to seek in the person of Miss Ella herself, by looking at her, some measure of the seriousness of the act. He found no mark of it upon her. The derangement of her brittle mind at this point moved him only to caution. He feared her insanity impersonally and indirectly, as a force out of control. Through instinct he gathered the fabric of himself tight into armor against it and through this act lost his fear, as a man locking his doors dismisses the thought of thieves.

Somewhere in the streets, after he had come from Miss Ella's house, he learned from listening to the voices of stragglers, men who out of conviction or cowardice themselves avoided involvement, that a mob was forming to lynch the Negro Dandelion. He was not aware of the full, possible meaning of the term, its potentials of error and debasement, but it struck him with a nameless and immediate terror, and he began to run. He ran in the sun-bright streets of Tilden, and the thing he knew darkened the day. He saw after a little that he was making his way toward the library where his father was assistant librarian, and he met men on the streets hurrying in another direction, going in groups or swiftly and alone, all toward Clifton Mills. He felt that the direction of their going was a deceit, that they were going for the Negro Dandelion. He could taste the knowledge in his mouth. The taste was that of terror and rust and he felt his joints watery with fear, but he ran. He had to reach his father.

"What's up, Boy?" his father said when he burst in upon him in the quiet reading room of Tilden Library. "What's up, eh?" His father always spoke as if anything could be taken for granted, as if nothing could surprise him.

"They're going after Dandelion," he said. He was panting. "They are going to get Dandy."

"Who?" his father said with the calm of incomprehension.

"Dandelion," he said. He repeated the name a second and a third time, as if it were necessary for identification.

"What for, eh?" his father said. He held a book he had been reading, his head was thrust forward and his chin elevated so that he could peer from under his horn-rimmed spectacles. The glasses gave his father's dark, handsome face a stupid, owlish look. "Why would they do that?"

"They are going to *kill* him," he said, and the terror in him rose racking in his throat like a sob.

His father turned suddenly and gripped his shoulders. "Now all of it, Boy!" he said in a taut voice. He told his father what he had heard in the streets of Tilden.

When he had heard him out, his father wheeled about and the corridor rang under the determined tread of his neat-shod feet. "Come *on*, Boy," he called to Farley where he stood rooted in the room, and swiftly the two of them went through the door and pounded down the street that led from the library to the center of town.

When they reached that, the square was deserted. No one moved on the streets that boxed the square, and his father stopped suddenly and stood on a corner, looking. The boy Farley could almost feel his father thinking. He had not spoken since they left the library, but his father's concern for the Negro transmitted itself to the boy. It was almost as if their own persons were threatened in the person of Dandelion, and something of the terror he must feel, if by now a hint of what was moving toward him by the back ways of Tilden had reached him, came to Farley and watered his blood. He stood by his father weak from the thoughts of it. Soon his father emerged from his brown study on the inconsequent corner, as if his plan of action were mapped, and they strode swiftly across the street and entered the courthouse that stood on its singular green plot in the center of the square. A musty odor of dust and tobacco juice met them as they entered the hall that bisected the building from south to north. Farley saw that his father's nostrils flared, and he snorted now and then to expel the sour scent from him.

On the right of the hall they saw the sign indicating the door of the sheriff's office, and under it on a small bronze plate the name. They entered without knocking and found a man sitting before a large oak desk. His father addressed the man. To the boy Farley he was only a portentous presence called Sheriff. He had not noted the name on the plate and did not know it, or if he did it was irrelevant. The importance of his office dwarfed the man and somehow consumed him into its entity, leaving him without any of his own though he was a burly man of six foot or over and had perfectly recognizable features.

"Morning," the sheriff said cheerfully, but his gaze glanced from theirs and would not hold. After a moment he asked, "What can I do for you?"

His father plunged breathlessly into the matter he was there about.

"I hear a mob is forming to lynch the Negro Dandelion," his father said and stood waiting, as if the news were sufficient to spring the sheriff from his seat like a jack-in-the-box and set him about his business of protecting a citizen.

"Well, now," the sheriff said. "I don't know about that. Where did you get the news?"

"The boy here," his father said.

"Well, a boy," the sheriff said, and he smiled at Farley as if to pre-pardon his error, "a boy might get it all wrong, don't you think?"

"No," his father said. "No, I think there is little chance of his being in error about a thing like that. Now if it were a lighter matter . . ."

The sheriff looked uncomfortable a moment. Then as if to propitiate his conscience he admitted, "Now I *did* hear something like that this morning." He turned a little away from them in his swivel chair. "But I was out checking up. Didn't find nothing to go on."

"This morning?" his father said.

"Ten, ten-thirty," the sheriff said.

"You saw nothing that looked like a mob?"

"No," the sheriff said. "Did see several men here and there. Two-three in a bunch. Nothing like a mob."

His father stood a moment as if weighing in his mind a fact of history before presenting it to his students at Tilden High. "What about this?" he said then, indicating with a sweep of his arm the square outside that enclosed them in emptiness and silence.

"Yeah, that square does look funny, don't it?" the sheriff said, and there was no sparring in his voice. His eyes betrayed a sense of dread, of expectancy of something he could not shape in his mind except in the outlines of catastrophe. It struck the boy Farley then that it was a strange situation to be in the dirty office in the bright August day, the three of them, menaced by the empty square. The sheriff's anxious hands hovered over the butts of his revolvers like nervous butterflies as he looked from his window into the square below.

"Those men I saw now," the sheriff said, "I followed some of them a good ways and they were going toward Clifton Mills. Every last one of them. Lots of men work there, you know. Change shifts all hours." He looked at Farley's father with something of relief, then went on, "The nigger lives on the other side of town. Plumb on the other side."

His father considered this as if he, too, were trying to wring relief from the news.

"That may be a dodge," he said.

"Yeah, it could be, couldn't it?" the sheriff said as if he were realizing it for the first time.

"It's your duty to protect a citizen, Sheriff," Farley's father said, looking hard at the sheriff.

"Well, what could I do, now?" the sheriff said. "Those men I followed. They may be up to something, I don't deny it, but you can't arrest a man for walking along the street no matter what you think he is up to." There was something of affront in his tones.

The boy's father considered. "Yes," he said, "I guess you are right," and he stood in thought for a moment. "We must save that man from a mob, Sheriff," he said presently.

"We've got to have something to go on," the sheriff said.

"But when it comes to a head so that we know what's taking place it will be too late," his father said.

113

Vast discomfort brooded in the sheriff's face. He spread his hands in a gesture of futility.

"Give me something to go on," the sheriff pleaded.

Farley's father wheeled in a quick, nervous movement as if he meant to catapult through the door, then he turned back again.

"You could arrest him," he said to the sheriff.

"Eh?" the sheriff said, as if he had not heard.

"You could arrest Dandelion and keep him in custody until the thing blows over."

The sheriff appeared to be considering. He made a sound in his throat that was negative, though he said nothing.

"You could arrest Dandelion and lock him up," the father of the boy Farley persisted.

"Yes, I could do that, I guess," the sheriff said in dubious tones, and his face was hard and set like a man's determined not to become involved in an explosive situation. "But nobody ain't made no complaint against him. I'd have to have a warrant."

"I'll swear out the warrant," Farley's father said quickly, "I'll do that."

"You think he is guilty?" the sheriff said. "If you think he is guilty. . . " he said, foreshortening the sentence in such a way that it seemed to dangle like a rope from some projection a little short of a man's length from the ground.

"No, no," his father said in exasperated denial, "but it is a way. Don't you see that it's a way?"

"Well," the sheriff said, "it's like playing with fire. I don't like it."

"Will you do it?" Farley's father said.

"I don't like it," the sheriff said. "If you do that and I arrest him a grand jury will have to indict him as charged."

"Will you do it?" his father said.

"As I say," the sheriff said, "it's as dangerous as a loaded gun."

"You could do it," Farley's father said. "We can prove to a grand jury he is innocent."

"It's a serious charge," the sheriff said.

"We could charge him with some other act."

"He was seen at the woman's house."

"As I understand it, he is there every day, he's employed by her."

"It's playing with the law," the sheriff said, as if he discovered all of a sudden a concept of the dignity and weight of his office. "It might get us both in a heap of trouble."

"Say whether or not you will do it," Farley's father said.

"Just look at it this way," the sheriff said. "If I bring him here and lock him up they'll come after him just the same. They'll come to my jail and take him."

"They might be stood off," his father said, but there was not much conviction in his voice. His knowledge of history was not limited to that of the kingdom of Thebes. He knew it could be dangerous as well as futile to try to counter a mob.

The sheriff said nothing. When the boy's father had suggested bringing the Negro to jail on a trumped-up charge his hands hovered suddenly over the butts of his guns and he looked quickly all about him once as if to forestall menace from some unexpected quarter.

The two men measured each other with careful eyes. The boy Farley saw his father's shoulders relax into stooped lines as he stood dejected in the center of the dirty office. He could feel the two resisting each other in the silence that overflowed from the square into the room. He could feel also that the sheriff was winning, not necessarily because his will was the stronger but because circumstance advantaged his will.

"If I could see Dandelion," his father said, as if to himself, and the voice of the sheriff pounced suddenly into the silence when he stopped speaking.

"What's that?" he said.

"If I could see him," the father of the boy Farley said, "if I could reach him before the mob does and get him away. Get him into the hills. He'd be safe."

"Why, sure," the sheriff said. "That's the thing to do. I'm sort of between a knot and a hard place myself. Nothing to go on." He was vastly relieved and he could not keep his relief from coloring his voice. His face cleared and his hands came away from hovering near the butts of his guns.

"Come *on*, Boy," Farley's father said. He hurried through the door and strode swiftly down the hall, and the boy followed hard on his heels.

The sheriff called after them. "I wouldn't worry about it, Professor. Do what you can. I got my deputies out. We'll do what we can." His voice at the last was coming faint over distance for they were out of the hall and halfway to the street.

When they had gone the sheriff sat in his office stroking his outthrust chin. He sat as if deep in thought a moment, then raised his hands before him and stared at the palms before folding his fingers forward and inspecting the nails. When he opened his hands again he placed them against the edge of his desk and half turned himself in his chair.

"Ed!" he called loudly in an irritated voice, and a man wearing the badge of a deputy sheriff entered from the next room and stood looking at his boss in sleepy, half-contemptuous deference.

"Ed," the sheriff said, "get on out there and tell them if

they want that damn nigger get him in a hurry. He's going to make trouble."

The man swung around without a word and left the office. In a moment his car spun from the square, going in the direction of Clifton Mills.

"Ah," the sheriff said, "the nigger lives on the other side of town." He opened a drawer of his desk, rummaged in it, and apparently finding nothing he wanted, slammed it shut with a vicious thrust of his arm.

# Part II

# AFTERNOON

# XX

THE INDIVISIBLE day is yet fractured into perceptible seg-
ments of time, seconds, minutes, hours, and as the crowd
began to gather at Clifton Mills the clock stated noon without likelihood of contradiction, for the men overstepped
their shadows as they walked.

Clifton Mills stood on the southeast edge of Tilden. Beyond it the mean dwellings of the poor frayed into the open
countryside. A triangle of streets enclosed the mill; on the
inner edge of the triangle, inward from the sidewalks, was a
tall hedge that reached almost to the height of the opaque,
repugnant blue windows that predominated in the spaces of
each wall. The hedge was breached on one side of the triangle by the mill entrance and on the opposite by a railroad
siding. The building itself was in the form of a huge T, with
the top of the T parallel to the main street. The space formed
between the angling walls and the hedge was sequestered,
and it was here the men of Tilden began to gather once they
had decided to lynch the Negro Dandelion.

The first of the men arrived from the center of the town.
At the apex of the triangle they left the main street that ran
by the face of the mill and reached the rear of the building
by a side street that intersected a cross street farther on. To
reach the open space of the mill yard the men had to thread

the hedge, and as they broke through the hedge with the risen sun to their backs their shadows went before them, short pygmy shadows that jerked over the cropped grass of the mill yard with a ridiculous mincing gait. With their eyes the men followed their cowering shadows, so that they all arrived a little way from the wall staring at the ground. When the men lifted their gaze again they avoided looking at each other. They assumed attitudes of waiting and stood in silence.

From the farther edges of the town cars filled with men began to arrive drifting into position behind each other with engines idling as they made a long file on the right side of the street. The noise of the tires braking to a stop on the loose gravel of the street's edge rasped along the nerves of the men already gathered inside the hedge and at each new arrival the men screwed their faces into masks of irritation. Still men on foot came sprinkling from the various sectors of Tilden and joined the men inside the hedge. Those first to arrive had formed a nucleus and the cluster grew by additions to its periphery. Soon the group began to move, the man at the center turning in an effort to see each new arrival at the circle's edge and each man in his place, until the whole mass was a great spring winding itself.

The coil of men in the mill yard continued to move for some time, now slowly, now with renewed momentum, until there were no new arrivals. Suddenly the man in the center, who had been one of the first arrivals, began to speak. It was as if by centripetal force he had been thrown to the center of the circle and by this given authority. His name was Harker, and he was a big, dark man whose voice rang resonant and deep, as if it came out of a well.

The first word he spoke was not a word. It was a heavy

raw command that sounded something like *Haak!* When
he spoke the circle broke immediately and spread unevenly
in the mill yard.

Just then the car of the sheriff's deputy pulled to a stop
by the others. The deputy got out and stood looking at the
men, who had become still and tensed like animals poised
either for flight or attack. The deputy read their faces, hesitated, then reassured by the nature of what he had to tell
them he approached the group with determination. The outer
edge held firm against him and by brigade, from mouth to
mouth, the word of the sheriff was passed to the leader in
the center, the man Harker. Without waiting for acknowl-
edgment the deputy got into his car again and drove away,
slowly, looking to left and right into the emptied or shaded
houses, as if on leisurely patrol.

"Are we all here?" cried the dark man when the deputy
had gone.

"All here!" cried the men.

"Who's got the rope?" Harker said. "Anybody got a
rope?"

"Ho!" said a man at the edge of the crowd, hefting a coil
of new plowline at arm's length above his head, "Enough
rope!" Laughter in basso and treble voices greeted the man's
words. But Harker lifted his hands and held them palms
down at the height of his breast for a long moment. The eyes
of the crowd fastened upon the stilled hands that remained
poised until they had drawn the last shred of sound from the
men gathered in the mill yard.

When all was silent, Harker pushed his hands downward
with a sudden violent motion and spoke:

"All right, let's go get him!" he said.

# XXI

THE BOY Farley and his father came on the Negro Dandelion before the mob reached him. On their way from the sheriff's office in the courthouse on the town square, the man's mind moved among history and came on the disposed forces of arms around the field of Waterloo. The morning of June 18, 1815, momentous with the event of battle yet pending, as the man knew from his reading of history, came on lowering and heavy. The rain that had fallen on the previous day had reduced to a thick drizzle which continued to descend until the day was considerably advanced. Because of the nature of the soil of that place, a deep clay soil covered for the most part with standing corn, the weather was disadvantageous and may have caused Napoleon's otherwise unaccountable delay in issuing the order to advance to his troops already established in battle stations by first dawn. The Duke of Wellington with characteristic vigor took advantage of this delay to further deploy his troops and distribute his spare ammunition to be ready for carriage to all parts at a moment's notice. Even so, in the morning it was yet too early to tell whether the continuing drizzle and the miry soil should work to the defeat of Napoleon and Grouchy or to Wellington and Blucher.

Before his mind had time to pursue the matter the man and his son were in sight of the Negro's house and the man's mind left off its concern with Waterloo and took up the matter in hand. The father of the boy Farley had little taste for what he was doing. He was not by nature a Samaritan. He felt that it was his duty to try to save the Negro Dandelion, to try to extricate him from the web which not justice but circumstance had woven about him. The thought was in his mind briefly that though in nature the spider and his victim are most often of a same darkish color, in this instance it was only the victim that wore the hue of the trapped fly. Too, the man had little conviction that his efforts on behalf of the Negro Dandelion would meet with any success; perhaps the mob would have come upon him already. But there was something in him, something foreign to the mob which would make it impossible for him to persuade or deal with it directly, that made him persist.

The chickens in the lot by the Negro's house set up a squawking as the man and his son approached. When they had passed the chicken pen of sagging wire they came on the Negro himself. He sat flat on the ground with his misshapen legs thrust out before him, his hands spread flat as if he were in the act of pushing himself up. Yet he did not rise.

"Listen!" the father of the boy Farley said as they approached the Negro. "There's a mob coming for you. They think you raped Miss Ella. You know what they will do to you?"

"Mr. John, I . . ." Dandelion began.

"No, now, listen!" the man said in a rush of speech. "You've got to get away. You've got to get up now and run.

Run into the hills, get out of sight. Quickly, before they come!"

"Mr. John," Dandelion said. He sat flat on the ground, his back against the sagging chicken coop.

"Are you going?" the father of the boy Farley said. "They'll be here any minute now." He half turned his head aside as if listening for the approach of feet.

"Mr. John . . ." Dandelion said. He shook his head as if to clear it. The boy's father waited for what Dandelion had to say but the Negro only sat in silence and said nothing.

"Or are you going to sit there like a damn fool and wait for them?"

"But, Mr. John," Dandelion said, and Farley's father waited for him to complete the sentence, but nothing came. The Negro sat looking to one side so that they had a view of the profile of the big vacuous face.

"Well, God damn you, then," the boy's father said angrily and turned aside with a swift nervous movement as if he meant to let it end there. But he turned back after a moment and glared at Dandelion as if he should like to hang him himself.

Dandelion saw the angry impatience in the face of the man and he turned away from him to the boy. "Mr. Farley?" he said in bottomless anguish, as if through speech he might somehow reach the boy and be less utterly alone. The boy Farley recognized the appeal, and he felt moved to respond in kindness but some force blocked his impulse, locking him off from any show of sympathy, and when he had repudiated the impulse he felt suddenly smaller, contracted in stature.

Because the man glared at him still Dandelion said:

"Ain't nowhere to go." Then he lifted his head a little and spoke defensively, "I ain't done nothing."

The man rocked back on his heels and stared at the Negro. It had not yet occurred to the professor of History at Tilden High to ask himself whether or not the Negro was guilty. At this stage the question was beside the point. The point was that the Negro's life was in danger. Not only that, he would surely forfeit it without benefit of trial unless somehow the mob could be thwarted. His mind moved among history, and what it caught at was King John at Runnymede on the middle day of June in the year 1215. He thought of the prerogatives the King relinquished there which became the rights the people had ever since retained. The man smiled a little bitterly to himself as he thought of these, for it was the Great Charter extorted from the King on that June day which undergirded the right of trial by a jury of one's peers.

He regarded the Negro, saw him docketed before a court of justice which should determine his guilt. The man shook his head, negating the likelihood of any such probability. Once the mob had come upon him it would not be interested in hearing evidence. It had already instituted what for its purposes was court, had heard evidence, or what passed as evidence, in the court of the common square, had pronounced him guilty and passed judgment. Now all that remained was to execute sentence of death.

"Look," the boy's father said, the urgency he felt hurrying his words, "get into the hills. You can hide there and escape. Look there now, there's only a hundred yards across the fields to where the woods begin."

"Naah," Dandelion said, and a stubborn quality came into his voice. "I ain't done nothin'. Ain't nowhere to go."

Farley's father made a gesture of impatience, but a tone of respect had come into his voice when he spoke.

"Of course you don't want to run away from something

you haven't done. I *wouldn't* run. But that's different. They wouldn't dare hang *me*, no matter what I had done. You've got to get away. You're a Negro."

"Mr. John," Dandelion said, and a spasm went through his misshapen legs, "I can't go nowhere."

"Eh?" Farley's father said, baffled, "why can't you go?"

"I can't walk," Dandelion said. He raised his buttocks from the ground with the strength of his arms and turned facing the earth and tried to heave himself to his knees, but his warped useless legs flung out of control in his dirty pantaloons, and he lay on his stomach supporting his upper body on his elbows.

"Oh, in Heaven's name!" the man exclaimed. He felt a burning and impersonal rage at the fate that should have stricken the Negro's legs useless when he needed them most. His mind, moving among history, came again to the disposed forces about the field of Waterloo and somehow he equated the fate of the Negro with that of the French forces: Soon after the first sound of musketry firing from the southwest boundary of the wood of Hougomont was heard, it began to be evident that the weather, the terrain, and inexplicable fate itself all favored Wellington.

The man as he stared at the Negro was stabbed suddenly by the small blade of pity. "We'll hide you here," he said. "Here, Boy," he said to Farley, "let's get him into this coop." They lifted and half threw the helpless Negro into the coop. He landed amongst the dried chicken dung and when he had righted himself with the strength of his arms he sat resting his back against a slatted wall. The coop was one the Negro had made himself. It was low and narrow, barely affording him room to sit upright.

"Come *on*, Boy," his father said to Farley who had shut

the warped door of the coop upon the Negro inside, making him less visible. The man turned back to Dandelion. "We'll see if we can stop them somehow. Keep out of sight now." He added the useless admonition without thinking about it. "I'll be back," he called finally as, followed by his son, he began to move away with long nervous strides.

"Thank you, Mr. John," the Negro said.

The professor's mind was already moving among history as they left the Negro's yard and approached the street; again it came to the contested field not far from Brussels, and identified itself with Ney and the little Corsican on the evening of that 18th of June, when the battle was over, and lost. It occurred to the man then that all battles are both won and lost, but as he stalked toward the street of no name that led by the Negro's house his mind did not know how to wring comfort from that platitude.

The boy Farley and his father had reached the street. Looking back they could plainly trace the outline of the sitting man through the slats of the coop.

"Mr. John!" the Negro called in a loud voice.

The man turned hurriedly and went back to the coop. "What is it?" he said.

"I dreamt it," the Negro said in a quiet voice.

"What?" the father of the boy Farley said. "How's that?"

"I dreamt it all," the Negro said.

"You mean you dreamed it all just like it's happening? Last night?"

"No, not last night."

"When?"

"All the time. I always dreamt it."

As the father of the boy Farley turned to go away again

the Negro, not looking after the man but straight before him as he sat in the chicken coop, said to himself: I wasn't asleep. I dreamt it all the time.

He had a great craving for a dip of snuff.

# XXII

THE SHADOW of the men gathering at Clifton Mills towered over the town and touched the Negro Dandelion as he cowered in the chicken coop a half mile away. He was aware of the shadow even before the visit of the professor of History at Tilden High. He felt it against his skin like a cast of cold, like the shade of a wood on a winter day. Now and then he shivered as he sat with his back resting against the end of the chicken coop and stared ahead. His poll with its mat of hair, though not touching it, felt the proximity of the top of the coop and he bowed his head a little. Mostly his hands lay vacantly upward in his lap, but now and then he clutched a slat on each side of the coop and his arms sagged downward like dead weights from his bent wrists. He could see out of the coop to either side well enough through spaces between the slats on a level with his eyes. He could not see out behind him because the coop was too close to allow of his turning of his body. Because of the angle at which his vision struck the coop directly in front of him the landscape outside appeared a scene of wood and sky heavily marked over with dark parallel lines.

Ole Mammy, Dandelion said to himself.

He ran his tongue over his dry lips. Nothing was in his mind but a dry heat, as if the atmosphere of the day had gotten inside his head. He could not think through it nor around it. He felt as if what he saw outside, the images of the mountains to the right of the town and the immediate street and houses and trees, got no farther into his head than the back of his eyeballs. Beyond that his skull was a hollow of dry heat.

Ole Mammy, Dandelion said to himself.

From the right side of the coop he could see almost to the top of the steps leading into his own house. Below them he could see a sliver of brown, bare yard. He looked at it only once and turned his head the other way. Ole Mammy, he said to himself without even resurrecting an image of her or thinking of what he had said. His mind was balled to a dry heat and his eyes reached into the town that lay to his left, straining after the first sight of the men.

They were not coming yet.

But that meant nothing because they were coming finally. It was this knowledge that made of his mind a cavity of dry heat. He could think of nothing to do, no way to save himself. When he would begin to think of what he would do, his thought took a divided path around the nether rim of his mind, and when it had got only a little way was withdrawn again to its starting point, both prongs of it regressing at once and at the same rate, like a serpent's forked tongue being drawn into its sheath. The block to his thought was that there was really no escape. Beyond him lay the hills and hiding; from the direction of the town the men would come. Though to him it was an unknown quantity subject to imminent qualification simply by their approach, there was still enough distance between himself and the men to allow of flight. But the space between him and the hills was a moat of distance he could not span because his legs were paralyzed and he had no other means of locomotion. It was this impassable space his divided thought encountered in its efforts to map for him a route of escape. Each time his divided thought retreated to its starting point it was an effort to plan a new strategy. His thought continued in its effort to extricate him from his impossible position, going on in its half circle of exploration, because he had not yet brought himself consciously to admit there was no escape.

Ole Mammy? he said to himself.

Nothing answered him. A little dust boiled in the yard, in a whirl of air. It moved toward the coop as if seeking him out but settled again short of his hiding place, and the landscape lay still and metallic under the glare of the sun.

Lapped by the heat the sun made in the closeness of the coop, at some time in the interval between the hour of his flight from Miss Ella's house and noon he slept. It is said that the man who lies down for the last time in a bed, in Death Row, as often as not sleeps soundly. The soldier endures the sound and fury of battle until the antennae of his senses become blunted to terror and, given the opportunity, he will lie down and sleep in the very lap of death. The child caught in misdeed drowses under the dread of the strap. He thought of none of these things, but while his death composed itself and took shape on the other side of town, drugged by the anesthetic of terror he drowsed and fell asleep in the coop.

While he slept he dreamed. The dream seemed to flow into him through an oval opening, a gateway of perception shaped something like an egg lying on its side. Or else he looked through this gateway into the dream country beyond. All the while he was dreaming his sleeping mind was troubled, as if it sensed somehow that something was wrong with the dream.

The first thing he saw through this gateway was an enormous world. Though the outer edges of it were blurred out of focus, it was not fragmented, nothing was missing. This world was rounded and complete and his sleeping mind, because he was not aware that there was anything beyond it to know, was filled with a sense of its completeness. The objects of the world he saw, or that flowed into him as if it liquefied to pass through the perceptive eye and then took shape again, seemed disproportionate. It was as if a man seen against the base of a tree that kept its appearance of normal height should appear no more than six inches tall. After a little this disproportionate view of things began to right itself and things began to take on their proper perspectives, and it turned out that the world had shrunk to a landscape, and it was one he knew. It was the known country of his childhood and there was a familiar house in it.

There was something in his sleeping self that greeted the familiarity of the dreamscape and he seemed to rest, suspended, in a peace that abrogated for an indefinite time, not long, the hold of trouble on his mind. When in the dream he grew aware again of the particularity of things the scene was still the same but there was a strangeness about it, as if the viewpoint had somehow shifted beyond the authority of a circle's 360 degrees and he looked at the house that might have been his own from a quarter from which he had never seen it before.

A figure came through the door of that house and began to play in the yard. The figure was that of a boy and it fell at once into pantomime, like a doll figure moved by strings. The actions were familiar to the sleeping man but he felt nothing of kinship with the figure because it was not lame. The dream boy kept his face averted or else the distance was too great for his features to be recognizable. The whole figure was obscure, as if shadowed, in sharp contrast to the light that framed the scene. That light had the same quality as summer sunlight which often tricks out in seeming immortal gear the commonest objects, a solitary tree seen as one passes a strange field, a filling station immovably wedged into the apex of branching roads.

The first pantomime actions of the boy were only the exuberant motions of play. After he had watched these a little in the dream, the agent of perception suddenly closed to darkness and the Negro Dandelion woke in the coop. He shifted his position slightly, easing himself, and slept again.

In the resumed dream the figure moved with marvelous ease through its pantomime actions. The motions were all known to the sleeping man's mind, to the very cords and tendons of his body. The figure might have been chopping wood, or wielding a hoe in a hot June garden, or beating a rug even, but that never in the yard where he was but before a house of quality. The figure pantomimed through its gestures, the arms lifting and falling without wielding an instrument, without sound. It only seemed to be demonstrating to the sleeping man how easy it all was, or how easy it might have been.

After a while the dream figure appeared larger, as if it had grown taller or was closer. Its exuberance had taken on a different quality, as of a change from within, secretive, glandular. The gestures were dancing and ritual, and for the first time the sleeping man was aware that the figure had spoken. He had heard nothing, but nevertheless he was aware of the word. Perhaps it had not been audible but translated into terms of light and motion which struck his sight rather than his ear. The word which seemed to him so undisputably present was the word love. The Negro Dandelion had never heard it, had never once heard it addressed to himself, but he knew what the word meant or should mean, or might mean, for he recognized it even though it had no sound.

As if the word were incantation a second figure was suddenly present with the first. It was a girl. His sleeping self saw that it was possible. The two figures were soon made equal, one, or the same, and their movements were synchronized and they lock-stepped away. Neither was the face of the girl clear. It was like Rhoda's grown older or the woman Angelicia's grown younger, and like neither's. But even in sleep he saw that it was a possible face.

The only thing else he saw was a field. If he walked there he walked in safety. If he was hungry there, since the field was beneficent he found food. He was no longer alone there, for this was a field full of folk. The field was the place of laughter and of the commonest things of his need. There was a part of the field, the farthest edge for its whole width, that was dark. He saw that in crossing the field one must come last to this edge of darkness, but in his dream he was only about halfway across it when abruptly the oval of perception seemed to rush toward him and grow smaller; and in it and through it he saw what it was that was wrong with the dream. It was an eye through which the dream entered or looked out, and the lid and the rim of it were not the dusky color of his own skin, but white.

He woke.

Naah, he said to himself.

It was not that he minded being alone. He had been alone almost since he could remember. Naah, he said, and his thought had almost completed the circle around the nether rim of his mind, making the admission that there was no escape. He had moved little since being placed in the coop, only turning his head from side to side in an effort to see out, but now he began to move, maintaining the gap between the separate branches of his thought that strove to meet around the dry cavity of his mind, in order to obey the command of the godhead of survival throned in his cells. Live, was the command, and he began to work himself frantically forward toward where the door was in the center of the coop. He inched himself painfully forward and when he was even with the door he leaned his torso through it. He placed his hands flat against the ground outside and began to twist his lower body free of the coop.

So intent was he that at first he did not hear the sound of approaching motors. When their drone struck him he grew suddenly rigid. After a moment he began to roll his eyes upward and to the side to bring the street into his field of vision. Only his eyes moved, rolled in a slow curve of terror to a dead-stop of recognition.

He saw the file of automobiles coming along the potholed street that led to his own door. They came with a certain air of sobriety and dignity, evenly spaced and at a moderate speed, almost like a funeral procession. Soon he could make out the figures of men behind the windshield of the lead car. His throat was unlatched and sounds came out of it, dark syllables of regret beyond the power of speech. Suddenly he was sick and he threw his head forward and retched, but nothing came from him but a little miscolored water that rose hot and viscid from his straining bowels.

# XXIII

THE SUN of noon struck the spire of the First Church of Tilden and lighted its tapering hexagonal surface everywhere
the same. The apex had only begun to cast a short shadow
down the east side of the cone when the professor of History
at Tilden High and his son Farley approached the square
of the town a second time. They had left the Negro Dandelion in dubious hiding on the outer edge of the town a short
while before. It was with the promise of help they had left
him, and the person to whom the professor's mind turned
first when he discovered the Negro Dandelion had been
stricken and could not use his legs to escape was the Reverend
Mr. Carhorn, pastor of the imposing stone church that stood,
as befitted its place of importance in the lives of the people
of Tilden, only a block from Mr. Darlington's bank which
occupied the central position of the south side of the square.

When the father of the boy Farley knocked sharply at the
door of Reverend Carhorn's study the minister rose from
drowsing in his chair and came forward swiftly for a man
of his advanced age. In a single motion he swung open the
door and extended his large, firm hand.

"I do not see you often, Professor," Reverend Carhorn
said. "Indeed, I do not see you often enough. I have had the
hope that you would become a regular member of my congregation. It is," he said, paying the father of the boy Farley

138

the compliment of recognizing his interest in history, "less festive than the worshipers of Dagon and Baal, less emotional than the converts of Wesley perhaps, but a fine spiritual congregation."

"Yes," the professor said. "Yes. No doubt I have been derelict of my duty in that respect." And it occurred to him for the first time in many years that this was true. His hand went out and rested for a moment on Farley's shoulder. It was a touch that recognized that he had failed his son to the extent of not habituating him in weekly attendance at the house of the Lord. Perhaps it was also a mute promise of repentance and reparation.

"But come in," the Reverend Mr. Carhorn said, as they still stood on the steps while he held the door ajar. He began to swing his big body about as if it were hinged to the door jamb and he was opening himself inward. He motioned for the two to enter.

"I wished to see you . . ." the boy's father began and then he hesitated while his eyes took in the interior of the study, then switched to the wall of the church that angled his vision from the cool retreat of the tree-shaded study toward the street.

A silence grew about them, and through it they heard the frantic drone of a fly trapped behind a window somewhere in the room.

"Yes?" said the Reverend Mr. Carhorn finally.

"Could we go into the church?" the professor said abruptly.

Reverend Carhorn retracted his large chin into his strong neck and looked at the man questioningly over the top of his glasses. "Ah, surely," he said, "but the study . . ." and he indicated the interior with his hand.

"Let's go into the church, into the sanctuary," Farley's father said. He did not know why he requested it. It seemed to him somehow that the matter he was there about should be broached in the church and not in the parson's study which had about it no more of the power of holiness than any common room.

"Surely," said the parson, and he joined them where they stood on the lawn and the three of them began to walk toward the door of the church that opened from the street. They walked the distance from the study in a silence that absorbed into itself the muted noise of their footsteps upon the grass and yet seemed empty of all sound.

As they walked the mind of the father of the boy Farley again moved among history. It ignored the records and chronicles of kings and battles and considered instead the intangibles of belief made tangible to see and sometimes to touch. It seemed he looked down a long avenue, an avenue paved with shells and with precious and semi-precious stones for divinity disdains to be approached by feet soiled by contact with the common earth. On either side of the avenue gods and idols were arrayed. First were totems and carved commemorative ancestral figures with inlaid eyes of haliotis shell. Next were figures of fowls and fish and animal figures, Assyrian bulls and rams; then primary gods and goddesses, Ra and Isis, the married sun and moon; and Buddha and Dagon and Baal, and Jupiter and Zeus. All of these and nameless others lined the avenue that terminated at a temple without icon, the shrine of the Unknown God. The lot of them, his mind saw, wore averted faces. Their craven eyes looked not at one but beyond, or were of blind stone; or like Buddha stared at the umbilicus that bore witness of his severance from mothering earth.

140

They were now inside the church and a dubiety of light hovered there, so that at first after they had entered they could scarcely see each other's faces. They drew close together in the central aisle and stood a moment under the darkness of the high ceiling where the shadows were unrelieved by the light from the stained-glass windows. The eyes of Farley's father were fastened upon a figure that stood central in a window behind the altar. The god of the shrine, he thought, the Unknown God finally made manifest wearing the face of man. The figure was that of Christ. His feet, touching nothing, supported His body above a pinnacle of blue, mountain or cloud, and His hands were outstretched in a gesture of supplication. Farley's father read into the aspect of the figure behind the altar this legend: Come unto me, all *ye* that labor and are heavy laden, and I will give you rest. . . .

The Reverend Mr. Carhorn had shut the door upon them when they had entered the church, as if he could shut out the world from encroaching upon the holy place by the closing of a door. He turned after a moment of standing in darkness and opened it again, and the light from the street entered and went down the aisle to the altar and reached no farther because of the angle at which it entered through the door. For a moment they all looked at the path the light took to the altar. *Thy path, O God*, the Reverend Mr. Carhorn said to himself. The boy moved his body out of the light and stood to one side in shadow. The boy's father stared shortsightedly through his glasses down the light's path. He had been unable to see anything in the shadowed church except the figures in the glass windows. What he saw now as if illuminated for this particular moment of revelation was a table standing before the altar. In the center of the table

stood a cross flanked on either side by money plates, the re-
ceptacles of offering.

"Yes," said the boy's father, as if he had his answer already
and not from the minister.

"You wished to speak to me about some matter?" the Reverend Mr. Carhorn asked gently.

Farley's father turned and faced the minister. "Yes," he
said. "It has come to me that a mob is forming with the in-
tention of lynching the Negro Dandelion. I was wondering
if you are aware of it." He asked it in a tone which implied
of course the minister knew.

The Reverend Mr. Carhorn rocked back on his heels and
swayed forward again, but by care his face revealed nothing.
What he was thinking was: Of course I know nothing of
any such matter. I would be the last to learn of such a matter
in any case. What do the people want of me except to be
the voice of conscience urging repentance? he asked himself, thinking of his congregation. Are you so blind as to
imagine that God is ever their accessory before the fact? he
shouted silently at the professor of History at Tilden High.
They dare not ask Him to strengthen their hand for fear
He will stay it; and I, he thought with a touch of bitterness,
am only a sponge to sop the blood from their conscience.
Though he was surprised by the news brought by the professor of History, out of some shame at not having been
taken into the confidence of his people, or out of an impulse
to cover up his inadequacy in the situation, he composed his
voice and told Farley's father a lie.

"I have heard a rumor to that effect," he said, belittling
the news, which he did honestly, for he could not bring
himself to believe that the people of Tilden who sat in his

congregation with such quiet hands could turn them to the lynching of Dandelion.

He had scarcely spoken the words when he was sorry for what he had done. Now he could not directly ask the professor for any details concerning the evil situation that had arisen in Tilden.

"May I ask what you have done about it?" the professor said.

"I have prayed," said the Reverend Mr. Carhorn, which was not true, but by telling the first lie he had forced the second upon himself.

"Of course," Farley's father said, "I would expect you to pray, but, begging your pardon, what else have you done?"

The Reverend Mr. Carhorn opened and shut his mouth without making a sound. Then he looked directly at the father of the boy Farley. "Nothing," he said.

"What do you propose to do about it?" the professor asked somewhat impatiently.

"Do!" said the Reverend Mr. Carhorn sharply, "what can I do? Shall I say mumbo jumbo and disperse the mob? Do you think it would work?" he asked bitterly of Farley's father. "You misjudge the powers of my office. I shall do little or nothing because there is nothing I can do."

The father of the boy Farley was beginning to realize that this was so, but the voice of the preacher was intoning above his thoughts.

"Do?" said the Reverend Mr. Carhorn. "I shall pray again and without ceasing, not for the saving of his body, for I misdoubt that God will save his body, but for the saving of his soul which He will surely save. Do?" he said again loudly drawing his strong chin into his neck, "I am going to let him be Stephen and be stoned, and be Paul and be persecuted, and be as Christ and be crucified. I am going to let him be the scapegoat of the Israelites and escape to the desert of death."

"Let him be Dandelion and be saved," the boy's father said shortly.

"He will be saved in the Canaan-to-come," the Reverend Mr. Carhorn said, drawing himself up. "We will escort him across the New Jordan into the Canaan-to-come. Like a lamb we will lead him."

"Like a lamb to the slaughter the mob will lead him now," the professor said, losing patience with the preacher's peroration. "They will hang him to a limb and no doubt torture him before they let him die. But he will die. Now."

"As the Lord wills," the Reverend Mr. Carhorn said.

The father of the boy Farley bared his teeth at the minister like a dog at another that covets his bone. "I will not believe it," he said to the minister. "The Lord wills the death of no man," he said, not knowing whether he quoted scripture or only stated his own belief. In that instant he rejected finally the idea of the differential works of God. This being so he realized all of a sudden that he was in the wrong place, for it had been out of some residue of irrational hope that he had come here. Was it his unacknowledged hope that by some mysterious feat of legerdemain the minister might really disperse the mob? He saw in his mind the image of an African conjure doll he had seen once in a museum and had to stifle an impulse to laugh. Then he was aware that the minister was regarding him sternly and speaking.

"Indeed God does not will the death of any man," the preacher was saying, "yet at the foundation of the world Tilden was scheming against the life of the Negro Dandelion. And Tilden will take the life of Dandelion because the world advanced as it advanced and not as it might have. At some point of turning, at some riven road, had the world chosen the better part then Tilden would not have taken the life of the Negro Dandelion, but would have said to his black face: O beggar, here, beggar, come sit by me, thy legs they are stricken, my legs they are strong. I will run for thee. Thy hands they are helpless, my hands they are whole. I will work for thee. But it is not so. If he must die, he must die. Across the New Jordan in the Canaan-to-come he will not be slain."

"In what time do we live!" the professor exclaimed. "In the time of the Amonnitish kings Moloch required his victim, but the victim was offered in the spirit of sacrifice and the immolators bore him no malice. His flesh burning was an incense of reverence. The God of Israel required only the flesh of the young lamb and the breasts of doves. He raised up Isaac from the altar in the bonded wholeness of his flesh and accepted the ram instead. To what god do the people of Tilden offer the foul and wasted body of the Negro Dandelion? To what god?"

"The time is now," the Reverend Mr. Carhorn said sternly, "and the god to which the people offer the body of Dandelion is the god of evil and destruction, and Satan and Beelzebub, and Siva and Cronus, yes, and death, are his names."

As the minister finished speaking the eyes of the father of the boy Farley were on the figure of Christ in the stained glass of the window. The figure was in perfect poise and at rest, and it occurred to the man all of a sudden that it was so and it would never change. The god of evil was living because he was nowhere enshrined except in the hearts of men.

He wanted then to be free of the sanctuary, and he

145

clutched his son by the arm and strode up the aisle to the open door and into the sunlight outside, leaving the Reverend Mr. Carhorn lost in prayer in the cool, faintly musty interior of the great stone church.

# XXIV

THE BOY Farley looked back once to see if his father watched him. He had been sent home to be with his mother but his mind veered away from their house on Maple Street and strayed through the quieted and empty town. The terror he had first known when he learned that the men meant to lynch the Negro Dandelion had been transmuted, since the threat was not against himself, into an overpowering curiosity as to what exactly the men would do to the Negro. He wanted to see and hear. When he was on the rise the street made a block or so from the great stone church from which he had just come he turned a second time and looked back. His father stood in the street with Mr. Darlington. Farley sat down on the curb and waited. When he looked again his father was gone. He had returned, the boy knew, to the library where his duty was, perhaps to pace out the rage of a man of good will bested by the forces of evil. The mind of the boy Farley pictured his father pacing a strict circle within the confining walls of the reading room, or brooding above an opened but unread book.

After a while the boy Farley got up from the curb and faced down Maple Street. He stood a moment regarding the maple-lined street, empty now except for himself. The maples stood in even files as far as he could see, breached here and there by store fronts and the entryways of dwellings. Here and there a roof towered above the maples, like castle turrets, he thought, and the whole scene rested in his mind in stillness and silence and of a sudden he remembered the story of "Sleeping Beauty."

Which prince, then, was he? he wondered as he began to walk. He walked with a preposterously deliberate stride for now he was not, as at morning, in pursuit of his pleasure. He was going where he had been sent. "If you follow them," his father had said, "if you go to witness it I will beat you. I have never beaten you, but if you go I will beat you." Except for his father's words he might have hurried now. He might be going in the direction of Jonathan's house, and once they were together they might . . .

But he was going home to be with his mother. Already he was within sight of the maple-screened mass of the woman Angelicia's house where it stood dominant above the walled garden just beyond Center Street. He could reach his own house as well if he turned right at the intersection and followed Center Street the length of a block, then bore left at the corners until he reached Maple Street again.

Not the jolliest prince, the boy Farley thought, seeking his identity within the framework of the story from his childhood. No laughter stirred the leaves of the maple trees. The town lay still in the fastness of the spell. He turned down Center Street and walked alongside the wall of the woman Angelicia's garden. When he approached the spot where the red tile-roofed summerhouse stood with its back to the street, the memory of yesterday's interim lived in his mind and suddenly he had a desire to see the place where they had buried the cat. He approached the wall directly behind the summer house and grasped the rough stones with his hands and swung himself up.

He clung by his belly to the wall a moment, feeling the

148

warmth of the sun-heated stone against his flesh, then he hunched himself forward and looked over into the close space behind the summerhouse.

He was so startled he almost fell forward over the wall. The Sleeping Beauty of the fairy tale lay in the space between the summer house and the wall of the garden. The figure was neatly clad in a light starched dress and it lay very still.

But it was only Rhoda. When he discovered this the confusion of time cleared in his mind, for it had been yesterday that he was Prince Charming and awakened her with a kiss and the more upon which the fairy tale never touched.

"Hello," he said at once and forgot the tale out of his childhood in the feeling of warmth for this creature of flesh and blood.

The eyes of the girl flashed him a frightened look, as if he had materialized the threat which hung over the town and directed it against herself. He saw relief grow in her eyes as she recognized him. Her body, arched tensely in her first fright, suddenly relaxed.

"Go away!" Rhoda hissed up at him.

"What are you doing?" he said, smiling down at her. He was very aware of the warmth of the stone against his belly.

"Go on," Rhoda said. "She'll see you. You'll make her find me."

"Who?" he said.

"Just go," she said.

"Tell me what you are doing first," he said. He swung a leg over the top of the wall and sat up.

"All right," she said in a tone of exaggerated resignation, "I'm hiding."

"What for?"

"Because I am," she said with the maddening perversion of logic to circumlocution common to the young.

"From her?" He meant from the woman Angelicia.

"Yes," she said. "Now go on," and she added suddenly and with conviction, "I don't like you anymore."

"Why?" he said. "Because we did?"

"Nothing's why," she said, refusing to touch with him the experience of yesterday.

He considered this in bafflement. His experience was not yet wide enough to divine how it was through the temptation that Eve's regard for the serpent suffered.

There was a silence between them. Three cats came from the garden into the space where the girl lay and sat looking at her with astonished and expectant regard. When they decided there was nothing for them they filed out again with a soft tread of determination so profound they did not even flick an ear backward when she called to them.

The harmony the sight of the boy Farley once made in her mind was absent when the girl looked at him.

"You don't make it anymore," she said suddenly to the boy Farley.

"Don't make what?" he said.

"Music. Bach."

"You sound crazy," he said.

Crazy! The word exploded in the mind of the boy Farley with all the attendant shock of a sudden loud noise. He thought then of Miss Ella, how she was crazy and why.

"You sound like Miss Ella," he said.

"I am Ella," the girl said.

"*Miss* Ella?"

"Ella is Ella," the girl said. He did not know whether she

150

played a game of pretend or made a more or less accurate equation of herself with one of her kind.

He pulled himself up and squatted on top of the wall. Then he swung his legs over and away from the girl and sat riding the wall sidesaddle. He entered once more into the question of the girl's change of attitude toward him, putting his query into a propositional conundrum.

"If I liked you would you like me?" he asked.

"No," she said. "You like the baby."

"Who?" he said.

"Baby Blond."

"Jonathan?"

"Yes."

"He's not a baby," he said.

"He *is*," she said with all the venomous emphasis of her dislike. "Why don't you let him? Why don't you let him nurse?"

"Maybe I will," he said.

She was sitting up in the space behind the summerhouse. He saw her dress was stained with earth where she had lain against it.

"You've ruined your dress," he said, all his interest in her suddenly transmuted into dispassionate observance.

"I don't care," she said with a flounce. "Aunt Angelicia will buy me another." She said it smugly. She had accepted her aunt in the role the woman Angelicia had designed for herself. "Aunt Angelicia will buy me anything," she said in both boast and belief.

"Why are you hiding from her then?"

"So she will find me," Rhoda said truthfully.

Faced with this paradox he swung suddenly off the wall

and left the girl in hiding. She had several hours to wait yet before Aunt Angelicia would be anxious enough to forgive her.

Not the cleverest prince, the boy Farley thought sourly to himself as he walked on down Center Street, reverting to the tale out of his childhood. If he had not promised his father. If he had said nothing he would not now be committed. He walked through the spell of quiet that still hovered over the witched town. He did not turn left at the corner beyond Angelicia's garden but continued on Center Street until he was near the street of no name on which the Negro had lived. His mind detoured around the shabby street where he had gone with his father to the futile aid of the helpless man, and he strayed and soon he was lost.

When he came to familiar ground again he saw that he was on the street that led to Jonathan's house. When he recognized this he began to hurry. It was quite a long way from Jonathan's to his own house on Maple Street, where he was going.

He turned from the street to Jonathan's door. No one was about in the garden that rolled green to the street, looking tangled and unshorn as if long neglected. The house when he reached it presented a shut appearance, like the others he had passed. The front door was a closed panel pressed upon from either side by equities of August heat.

He knocked at the door and Jonathan's mother met him there. He saw that her face was stilled by a certain constraint as if of unknowledgeable dread. Her eyes that were usually frank and gay like Jonathan's were somber and guarded. The mystery of the stilled town charged her person. She glanced beyond him to the street as if menace might lie in ambush there before she bid him enter. When he had gone through the door she shut it again, shut it against the weather of catastrophe that brooded in the empty street.

"Jonathan is out back," she said and he went through the house and into the yard. Jonathan lay on the grass full in the light of the August sun. He wore nothing but shorts and his skin was tanned the color of saddle leather. The so-blond hair, like corn silks in a windy field, was stirred continually in the light breeze, creating about his head the illusion of constant motion, as if he ran a race.

"Hi," Jonathan said in his equable voice, smiling his instant and luminous smile.

He was going home to be with his mother, but the moment he saw Jonathan he was certain he must see the lynching. They must see it together.

# XXV

A LITTLE before the professor of History at Tilden High left the Reverend Mr. Carhorn kneeling in the sanctuary of the great stone church, Mr. Darlington summoned his second vice-president to watch the tellers while he made a discreet excursion into the streets to see what he could learn about the odd circumstance that had emptied the square of the town and left the bank inactive, like a piece of machinery made idle because the raw material that poured into its maw to be transformed in its noisy interior into shapes strict and foreign had ceased flowing from its source. The ponderous bulk of Mr. Darlington advanced itself up the street with easy and deliberate tacking from side to side, like a ship navigating a channel against the wind. As if he could not manage to bring the whole weight of his body straight forward at once, he advanced half of his body and poised it on the tremendous pivot of his leg while he brought the other half equal with the first, where it rested in equilibrium an instant before taking the lead in the seesaw of his stride.

Mr. Darlington noticed as he walked through the August day that the sky seemed to hang perpendicular from the zenith to the hills in the west. It was of a transparent greenish color, textured like plate glass. It was, Mr. Darlington thought, as if the sky fronted the great bank of the world, and that image was not too large to house M. Darlington's concern with his occupation; he always felt somewhat cramped in his activities by the smallness of the town of Tilden. Ah, well, he was really part of the financial machinery that geared contemporary life and time. He was a vital cog in a vast machine, and though there were innumerable other cogs the breakdown of one, of his own bank, would affect the power of the whole machine. All the gear wheels intermeshed.

Of vital importance, Mr. Darlington thought, and he was thinking of himself and his bank. Indeed, of vital importance. The power that moves the machine of industry.

The August sun smote Mr. Darlington and he began to sweat. He paused in his tacking up the street to wipe his high broad brow with an immaculate white handkerchief. In his pause he gazed ahead of him up the street and saw the figure of the professor of History at Tilden High approaching. As Mr. Darlington recalled, his name was John Gaines, a person he himself had troubled to recommend to the school board, of which he was chairman. A competent person, thought Mr. Darlington, highly competent, but there seemed to be something distraught in the man's stride as he approached.

"Ah, Professor, good afternoon," Mr. Darlington said when they had come abreast of each other.

"Good afternoon," the professor of History said, "good afternoon to you, Mr. Darlington." He was on the point of hurrying past the banker. He was in no mood for platitudinous talk but the other was planted directly in his path and nothing short of a crane could set that tremendous bulk at nought and shift it aside.

"Hot," Mr. Darlington said, mopping his brow, and in a moment he continued in his slow, ponderous speech. "Pardon me, ah, but you seem somewhat distraught, Professor. Any trouble?"

"Yes," said the father of the boy Farley, "now that you mention it, trouble enough."

"Well, sorry to hear it, Professor. Something I can do to help?"

Farley's father looked at Mr. Darlington sharply from under his knit brows. When he had come from the parson he was convinced that no one would help him save the life of the Negro Dandelion. The thought was painful to him, and now he began to speak to the banker in a tone of bitter raillery.

"Yes," he said, "I believe you can help. You are the master of both those who buy and sell, in a manner of speaking."

"In a manner, yes," Mr. Darlington said, locking his arms behind him by grasping a great elbow in each hand.

"Then you should be able to help me," Farley's father said, "either way."

"So?" said Mr. Darlington.

"So . . ." Farley's father began, but what he said next startled even himself, "sell me a bucket of blood."

Mr. Darlington rocked in ponderous surprise. He widened his eyes at the professor of History as if he thought him crazy.

"*Professor* Gaines . . ." Mr. Darlington began.

"Or buy me a bone," the professor of History interrupted, "approximately eleven inches long by an inch and a half in diameter, somewhat flat in shape, not round, tooled at either end to receive a fitting of most precise measurement. Buy me a bone for a forearm."

156

THE HAWK AND THE SUN

"Professor Gaines," Mr. Darlington said, "I took you to be a man of reason. I am a commercial intermediary, so to speak. I do not know what all this foolishness is about, but I am not in the business of buying or selling blood and bones. They have, shall we say? no commercial value."

"No?" said the father of the boy Farley in a deadly quiet tone.

"Ah, no," said Mr. Darlington, beginning to stare at the professor coldly.

Anger mottled the face of the professor of History. He suddenly hated the banker with a fierce, irrational hatred because all the wealth of his bank could not restore or replace a single living cell.

"I expected you to say that," the professor said. "But are you not wrong, Mr. Darlington? Are you not altogether wrong? Is not the wealth of your bank the measure of the commercial value of blood and bones? Was not the wealth in it built up out of the spending of the one and the endurance of the other? Or, tell me, did a steel girder labor in the brickyards and come home and deposit its weekly pay check at your little wicketed window? Or did a clay statue wetted with water endure labor in the stave mill until the clay cracked and the water was too sluggish to flow, to die and leave an inheritance of exactly five hundred and forty-one dollars and five cents marked on the ledger of your assets?"

"I am a simple man, Professor," Mr. Darlington said. "I do not understand."

"You are also a poor economist," Farley's father said, "if you do not know that all wealth is from capital invested in labor which makes its return to capital by producing goods. You agree?"

"Of course," Mr. Darlington said, "but . . ."

157

"The body of man is capital also. It is invested in the labor that produces wealth."

"I see," Mr. Darlington said, but coldly.

"It reaches at some stage the point of diminishing returns and it is finally exhausted, but it has produced goods, towards which end it was invested."

"Yes, yes," Mr. Darlington said, and the ponderous bulk of him began to sidle away from the father of the boy Farley. The fine points of economic philosophy profited him nothing. He could not invest them at six per cent interest.

"As an investment the body of man has a commercial value and in the nature of such should be negotiable through a commercial intermediary, don't you think?"

"Possibly, Professor Gaines," Mr. Darlington said, and by now the whole mass of him was aroused almost to motion.

"I have a life to sell," Farley's father said. "How much will you give me for it?"

"Your own?" Mr. Darlington said doubtfully.

"No, not my own, but a life. What am I offered?"

"Well, really, Professor Gaines," Mr. Darlington said, as if this were a huge joke and he was willing to enter into the spirit of it, "I am not in the market for a life this morning."

"Or I would mortgage it to you," Farley's father said. "And at a good rate of interest. I'd make it commercially a good investment."

"See me some other time, Professor Gaines, and I may be in the mood for such a transaction. This is not the day for it, really. In the first place it is infernally hot here on the street. Shall we go to my office?" And he turned himself, swiveling his ponderous bulk slowly around, and set half of his body forward in the seesaw of his stride.

"Mr. Darlington," Farley's father said in a changed tone,

"your depositors are going to lynch the Negro Dandelion. I have done my best to prevent it. I have had no success. I suppose you can think of no way to stop them." No profitable way, he thought silently.

"So that's what this means?" Mr. Darlington said, arresting the great bulk of his body in its turn and indicating the empty square with his enormous hand. "No. I can't stop them. I make it a policy never to meddle in the private affairs of my depositors." His voice was cold, remote and withdrawn; he spoke in the tone he used to deny a loan to a man he considered a bad financial risk. "No, of course I can't stop them," he said and began to hurry as fast as he could toward the bank. In his hurry his body lost its usual ponderous dignity, but he was willing to forego it since no one was on the streets to see except the crazy professor of History at Tilden High.

Farley's father stood still a few moments, contemplating the receding back of the banker. "Shinbone and thighbone and fingerbone and footbone, a sack full of flesh and a bucket of blood. They are worth nothing. Nothing at all!" Then he raised his head and laughed aloud. It was a terrible sound. An indefinable change charged the whole air, as if it shielded from the sound its immaculate honor, and suddenly chastened the man struck his palms together with a sharp swift movement and began to walk.

# XXVI

From Clifton Mills the mob moved directly to the house of the Negro Dandelion. It passed in long file within a few blocks of the town square where the father of the boy Farley stood in effectless conversation with Mr. Darlington, the banker. When the men reached the Negro Dandelion's place they went first to the house itself and a group of them entered, in violence, while others ringed the house to cut off the Negro should he attempt to escape. Thus, or so they thought, they had their quarry in a trap, and it was the secret hope of some of the men on the outside that the Negro would break suddenly from the house, for they longed to shoot him with a charge of birdshot, though of course in the lower body where it would not be immediately fatal. He was due for a hanging.

The men on entering the one-room shack found nothing but the disarray of an ill-kept house. The Negro was not there.

Gone!

They began to pick up objects in the house and smash them against the floor and walls. Someone threw the Negro's cheap alarm clock against the cracked iron stove.

The clock protested with a feeble rattle of the alarm bell as it rolled against the wall. The works were broken and the hands stopped, fixing time in rigor mortis above the dented face. The scant crockery of Dandelion's cupboard soon lay sprinkled on the floor where it had fallen in a shower of dingy shards. A stout tall man picked up the single chair that stood as the Negro had left it that morning, at half-face to to grease-spotted table without a cloth, and sent it crashing against a wall. A leg of the chair flew free and caromed from the wall, striking one of the men on the shoulder. For a second the two men stood looking meanly at each other and suddenly the man struck by the flying chair leg shot out his fist and connected solidly with the tall man's jaw. The man fell, clutching at air. Before he could rise from the floor the bed was overturned and it pinned the fallen man beneath it by the upper body. His curses came muffled from beneath the odorous, foul bedclothes while his legs kicked in the air eloquent wild strokes of fury.

By the time the tall man had extricated himself from beneath the bed the group had gone laughing and cursing from the house, rocking it in their violence. When they came outside again they stood poised near the broken door looking this way and that, deciding, since the Negro was not in his house as they had expected him to be, what to do next. On the exit of the others the men who had ringed the house broke circle in the yard back of the shanty and withdrew again to the front to stand flanking the entering party on either side.

"Where's the nigger?"

"Gone!"

"Gone?"

"Gone, by God!"

161

There was a moment of silence in which no one spoke. Each listened for a sound that would betray the presence of the Negro. In that intense silence of listening they could hear nothing but the drum of their beating blood. Then the chickens in the lot, disturbed, set up a cracked, chortling chorus.

A hundred feet or so from the poised group the Negro Dandelion lay half out of the chicken coop. Since the arrival of the men he had not moved. He kept his eyes on the ground, assiduously avoiding looking in the direction of the men, as if not looking at them made his own body invisible, impossible to be seen. It was a ruse he imitated from the lower animals and if he had thought about it he would have had no faith in its efficacy. The ruse was the effort of the organism to preserve itself and went beyond the authority of the man's thought. Dandelion was not thinking anything. He was enduring terror-lengthened time and the effort was so intense it made his heart thunder loudly in his ears and his body break into an excessive sweat. Except for straining to hear the first indication of his discovery by the men, his attention was vised upon the chords of his neck which had begun to ache from the strain of remaining rigid. He must move his head soon to relieve the strain.

Their eyes drawn toward the lot by the sound of the startled hens, several men saw the Negro Dandelion at the same time.

"I'll be God-damned," someone shouted, "the old black rooster's already cooped!"

At the cry of discovery the Negro collapsed against the ground. The mob came toward him, breaking, despite the quarry cornered, into the pumping strides of chase.

From his position on the ground it seemed to the Negro

Dandelion that he looked up a tremendous distance into the faces of the mob, as if he were seeing them from the bottom of a well. The faces swam in his vision, in broken images, and became one great cruel, leering, violent face. He moved his spittle-flecked lips and spoke to the mob-face above him.

"I ain't done nothin'," he said.

"Stuck your black . . ." the mob-face said.

"No, please," Dandelion said. "I ain't done nothin'."

"Stuck your black stick . . ." the mob-face said, but he interrupted its speech again before it could frame the specific charge.

"No I ain't," the Negro said, "I ain't done nothin' a-tall."

The mob did not believe him. It bent its great face above him and leered at him.

"Raped Miss Ella," the mob-face said, "you black son of a bitch."

"Please . . ."

"You been in bed with a white woman."

"No, I ain't," Dandelion said. "I ain't raped Miss Ella a-tall."

"Wait a minute," a man said, "there's something wrong with this." Then he turned and spoke to the Negro. "Stand up. You think we come to set around for a chat?"

"Please," Dandelion said, "I can't stand up." He still sat flat on the ground leaning backward a little, resting against his spread hands.

The man who had spoken reached down and hauled the Negro to his feet. When the supporting hands were withdrawn the Negro's legs buckled outward at the knees like large parentheses breaking at the center of their curve, and he fell. After a moment he regained his sitting position.

They let him remain sitting then, but the face at the top

163

of the well was more antagonistic than before. When he denied a second time that he had raped the bookish spinster Miss Ella, the toe of a shoe caught him in the back, striking him over the kidneys with a flat, dead sound. His body surged suddenly forward from the force of the blow, his splayed hands ploughing short tracks in the dirt. He sucked in an agonized breath of air and expelled it but the pain of the blow remained like a blade in his flesh.

"Dispute the word of a white man, will you?" the man who had kicked him said.

Before he could straighten or speak he was struck again, by someone who stood in front of him. He saw the rough shoe on the foot that kicked him only as a brown blur and before he could move it struck him in the face and seemed to explode in a flash of light. For a moment Dandelion's senses quitted him. The blow caught his lips against his teeth and numbed them. A slow trickle of blood coursed from the corner of his mouth and dripped from his chin.

"That's for telling a lie," a voice said from the top of the well.

When he could manage his lips again he tried to explain, speaking hurriedly in order to discharge his obligation so he might remain quiet.

"I ain't done a thing," he said. "I just built Miss Ella's fire. She done sick already. That's the truth. I already told you all the truth there is. I ain't got nothin' to tell no lie about."

For the impudence of defending himself the mob rewarded the Negro with a rain of blows. His body, fluid above the dead waist, gave before each blow and struck repeatedly it presented the appearance of an animated rag doll contorting to match the frenzy of some inner ecstasy. The Negro's senses began to wander, reeling on the edge of unconsciousness, a fathomless depth a level below the well-like depth from which he looked upward into the mob-face. He had a desire to fall into this depth of darkness below the level of consciousness, but the rope of pain that promised to pull him under was snagged over some projection, the power of his body to endure.

"Wait," a voice said, and looking up the Negro Dandelion saw that the mob-face had spawned out of itself a new face, a face like its own but different, kinder. "Maybe he's telling the truth."

A gape of astonishment broke in the mob. For a long instant all things seemed suspended, even the day seemed fixed against space, secured by the silver nail of the unmoving sun. Then the hens in the lot chortled and a hawk rose from some invisible perch directly behind the Negro Dandelion's head and circled upward in a strong spiral of flight.

"You going to believe the word of a nigger before a white woman's?" the mob-face said to that other face when it had found its voice. "You going to believe a God-damn nigger?"

The new face, which was square and stern with strength, spoke then.

"I am going to believe him."

On hearing its speech the Negro's head came level, and he looked then at the mob from the height of a sitting man and no longer from the depth of a well.

The singular face which the mob-face spawned out of itself belonged to the farmer Abraham. He did not know exactly why he believed the word of the Negro Dandelion. Perhaps it was because it is given to the tongues of men sometimes to speak the truth. It might have been because none of Abraham's sons had ever told him a demonstrable lie.

The defection which the mob discovered in itself weakened it for a moment but soon it began to heal itself with wrath. "You had better go," the voice of the mob said to Abraham who when he took upon himself the assumption of the Negro's innocence assumed also his peril. "You are not with us," the voice said. "You believe a nigger before a white woman. You can't stand with us."

The farmer Abraham began to move away from the mob. He moved without fear but with slow, deliberate care from the menace that had shifted momentarily from the Negro to himself. Once he stopped and spat in the direction of a man who covered his movements with a double-barreled shotgun. The man, meeting Abraham's eyes, colored and flicked his gun barrel away from him.

Even as he moved away from his peril Abraham was aware of the hawk. It circled through the upper field of his vision, climbing steadily, as if in an element more stable than air. The hawk rose in widening circles and soon the periphery of its flight was totally beyond Abraham's vision.

When he could no longer see the hawk Abraham turned his undivided attention back to the mob. It followed him with sullen eyes. He glanced once at the Negro Dandelion and saw that he was no longer afraid, only weary and anxious. It occurred to Abraham that Dandelion's anxiety was no longer for himself but for the men, that in violating him they should violate themselves also.

Abraham turned his back to the mob suddenly and strode away down the street of no name.

When he had gone the mob was whole again in its triple body of cruelty, lust and wrath. It turned itself toward the Negro Dandelion and with impatience began to gather up the slack that had allowed the event of his execution to slew about indecisively.

At this point the dark man Harker began to give orders, speaking in a heavy voice of easy authority to the others. Quickly then a rope was placed over the Negro's head. The mob had meant to lead him to the place chosen for his hanging like a dog on a leash. It only added to its wrath that it could not inflict this indignity upon the victim because his legs were paralyzed and he could not walk. A man clutched him by each arm and the two, supporting his upper body between them, began to drag him along. His useless legs trailed on the ground. Soon his shoes were scuffed from his feet and the flesh grew raw and began to bleed. The Negro, because there was no feeling in his lower body, took no note of this, and neither did the men. Resting now and then, and often switching teams, they kept going and going.

They were carrying him into the hills.

# XXVII

FARLEY and the the blond boy Jonathan followed the men
into the hills. From Jonathan's house they went to the
Negro's house by the street of no name. Here they could
trace only to the street's edge the sign of the foray in which
the Negro was taken, but the two followed along the street,
by the route the men had gone, though the pavement bore
no sign of them, which had earlier been the way taken by
the people who wore the face of darkness in their Exodus
from the town of Tilden. As they left the Negro's place
they skirted the parked cars which had brought the men and
now waited with dead, metallic patience for their return. It
struck the dark boy that the cars were like the shells of enormous beetles whose live entrails fared voraciously elsewhere
and would return to reanimate their immobile armor. This
thought still occupied his mind when they picked up the
sign of the men again. The unpaved road which the street
became a hundred yards from the Negro's house had been
heavily trampled, and something which had dragged left
visible marks as roughly parallel lines in the dry dust of the
road. Now and again whatever had dragged had dislodged
small stones which lay overturned with the damp marks of
earth still on them. After a while Farley and the blond boy

found a scuffed shoe, and then another. When next they saw them the parallel lines were etched in the dust like marks made by dragging something rounded, and farther on they saw stones tinctured by the dark unmistakable color of blood.

When they saw the first discoloration on the stones they stood together in the road and shivered in the heat of the August day, which had tipped from the zenith of noon and now slanted toward night.

When I see the blood, the blond boy thought, looking at the discolored stones, and he remembered the Reverend Mr. Carhorn's text that had animated his mind on his passage through the morning town. Then the text had been only a dark meaning. He had expected nothing from its adverbial condition, but now it had come to pass and was a promise, of what he did not know. He felt only that the answer was imminent and lay perhaps with the dark boy who walked by his side as they took up the spoor of the Negro Dandelion and the men again.

Several hundred yards from the ended pavement the men left the street of no name and took a trace that led into the wooded hills to the west of the town. Because of the fear which they drew from the atmosphere of threat that pervaded the day, Farley and Jonathan left the road and as in a game of scouts and Indians began to stalk through the brush alongside. Now and then they entered the road to examine the spoor of footprints and bloodied stones. When it began to lift into the hills they cautiously kept to the road for fear of losing the trail. They almost lost the trace in the dry leaves at the point where the men with their victim had left the road and gone into the woods.

When they had found the faint trace in the leaves they

followed it up a small hollow that led to a bench of ground on Hester's Ridge. After they had gone only a little way from the road they were within earshot of the men. When they heard voices they stopped.

As they stood listening, over the sounds of the men the boy Farley heard the words of his father in his mind: If you go to watch it I will beat you.

"Let's wait," he said to Jonathan.

"What for?" Jonathan said. His equable voice betrayed no fear. When I see the blood, the blond boy was thinking and his mind left Farley and went on ahead to the imponderable scene where the men and the Negro were.

"They might see us," Farley said, and then, as if this were insufficient reason, he added, "we might have to tell about it." Suddenly then the dark boy understood the business about the Three Wise Monkeys. The first two monkeys took their elaborate precautions in order that the third might avoid turning informer.

He met the challenging gaze of the blond boy, and they went on in silence. Before they came in sight of them they stopped again and listened to the rowdy, raucous voices of the men. A sound came to them as of a plank struck with leather, a flat sharp sound which they could not identify, and when they heard it they looked at each other with the wide, frank stare of fear. Then they began to make a circle around the men to come above them onto higher ground. They went with the taut, slow-motion strides of stalkers, and with great care lest they dislodge a stone to go bounding down the side of the ridge and discover their presence to the men. After a little they came to a point on the steep spur of Hester's Ridge a hundred yards or less above the bench of ground where the men were. The low undergrowth hid them from the men. By staring through openings in the brush they could see all that went on below them.

From their perch on the steep slope Farley and the blond boy Jonathan looked down on the rite of execution the mob made of the Negro Dandelion's death, to their view a preposterous pantomime enacted in half-silence because of the distance from which they watched. They had been closer to the men in the hollow where they first heard voices, but from there a rise of ground hid them from sight. Now they could see but not clearly hear, except occasionally a loud, detached profanity or a high-pitched peal of laughter, and twice the peculiarly terrifying dull thud of a club struck against flesh. The men with the Negro had preceded them into the hills by an hour or more and by now they were tired of sporting with their victim. It was about time to finish it. Their movements as they circled about the Negro were quickening, as at the climax of a dance.

"Look!" Farley whispered to Jonathan. It was not to the action of the men that he called attention, but to the body of the Negro.

"What?" Jonathan whispered.

"Look how it is!" Farley said under his breath.

"I can't see it," Jonathan said. The bodies of the men that made a moving circle about it just then obscured the black bundle swinging by a rope from a black oak limb.

"Now!" Farley whispered, staring himself through the circle which had broken at the body of the Negro Dandelion. He saw that it was shockingly misshapen. The upper legs were like withered parentheses enclosing near the top where they joined the heavier darkness of the trunk the swinging sign of the Negro's manhood. The knees were large knots of bone and the shrunken lower legs grew from

these like the handles of mallets. Yet for all its grotesqueness
the body had about it its own integrity, a bond of wholeness
bruised here and there where it had suffered the violence of
the men. The boy understood on seeing the body how the
Negro's lameness, evidenced down all the streets of the town
as the Negro had walked there, resulted from the deformity
of his legs. Except for the deformity, and the bruises and the
blood which were only darker splotchings at the distance
from which he beheld them, the body was not demonstrably marked by any sign of commission.

No mark, the mind of the boy Farley said, and suddenly
he was a disbeliever in the branding of Cain. His thought
went then to the blond boy and he acknowledged at last
what was possible, what the absence of brand upon the body
of Dandelion made so.

Farley turned then to look at the blond boy. He saw that
Jonathan was not watching the men; his eyes were closed
and he leaned his head against the rough bole of the dogwood bush by which he crouched. His little bones, Farley
thought, but the memory of the knowledge his hands had of
the blond boy was broken as a cry that was like a bestial
command came from below. He looked downward again
and saw that the circle about the Negro Dandelion had
stilled and a man approached the swinging body alone.

It was difficult to see what went on below, and the boy
Farley shuffled a little closer on his knees to see better
between the leaves of his screening bush.

"They cut him *there!*" he said to Jonathan when he was
certain of what had happened in the circle below them.
"Did you see them? Did you see them do it?"

Jonathan lifted his head to look, peering around the bole
of the dogwood tree.

"Did you see them?" Farley urged as if he needed corroboration to establish belief in what he had seen.

"No," Jonathan said in a throaty whisper, "cut him where?"

"*There!*" Farley whispered in a voice of awed outrage. He turned and looked at Jonathan and their eyes met and glanced away in evasion.

"But where?" Jonathan said. The men had begun to move again and he could not see the body of the Negro.

Farley turned and stared at Jonathan's crotch where his pants were drawn tight in squatting and Jonathan followed the direction of his gaze.

"Oh," Jonathan said. "Oh!" he said again and understanding was in his voice which came in a throaty whisper. He hunched himself forward on his heels in order to see better between the boughs. He was so close to the other now that his warm breath touched Farley's skin like the intermittent tread of flies.

The mob below had broken, the men moving away. Together Farley and Jonathan stared at the body of the Negro. It was not different from before except that the dark parentheses no longer enclosed the sign of its manhood. Instead there was a pouring of liquid stain that flowed down the mummied legs and caught the light and shone.

"When I see the blood," the blond boy said aloud.

"What? What is it?" Farley said. He saw that the blond boy's face was drawn and he was shaking. They clutched each other then and lay clinging together in fear as the men left, making a noise in the leaves as they went like a herd of beasts in frantic stampede.

# XXVIII

FROM THE stilled circle of men on Hester's Ridge the man Harker who appointed himself leader of the mob in the mill yard had detached himself and approached the body of the Negro Dandelion alone. He held a hunting knife in his hand and while he moved toward the suspended body he tried the edge of the blade against the ball of his thumb. It would do; on occasion he had clipped hairs with it. Behind the man Harker the mob waited, silent and intense.

The breathing body of Dandelion swung like a filled sack tied about the middle at the end of the rope. When they had brought him to the bench of ground on Hester's Ridge they selected a black oak tree with a stout projecting limb for his hanging. As it happened they had to hang him from the limb in a truss. They had meant to adjust the rope which was about his neck so precisely that the Negro could avoid strangulation so long as he stood on tiptoe, and after they had had their sport with him, hang him properly. The fact that his legs were paralyzed forced them to alter their plans. They devised a substitute. The rope which they had placed over his head at the chicken coop by the street of no name was secured to the black oak limb. A second rope was tied about his body, under the arms, and he was hefted up until three or four feet of slack occurred in the first rope. Then the second rope which supported his body and allowed it to swing like a pendulum was secured to the limb. At the last they would cut the second rope and his body, falling, would be brought up short by the first rope which would break his neck or strangle him.

The dark man Harker heard the rustle of the mob behind him as he approached the Negro's swinging body. He was almost within arm's length of it now and he regarded it with an intense stare. By now it bore innumerable gashes and pricks where it had been knifed by the circling men, and the blood and the sweat of anguish had dyed it an ominous hue. It was entirely naked and for a moment the dark man felt again the shock which had rocked his senses on first beholding the Negro's malformed nakedness.

As soon as they had him strung up they ripped away the Negro's clothes. When he was naked they saw that the upper body was sound except for the bruises that had been dealt it beside the street of no name. It was the deformed lower body which held them in staring fascination. They stared at the crooked legs, shrunk to the misshapen bones of shin and thigh and hung about with loose skin as wrinkled as a mummy's, and for the moment of their regard all stood maimed in their lower members.

"My Christ!" a man said. In sudden resentment of his deformity, the man thrust the blade of his pocket knife into the Negro's flesh to its full length. When the knife was withdrawn a single drop of blood, globed like a drop of water on oil, rolled mercurially from the shining blade.

After that first thrust the men had circled the body of Dandelion for an hour or more. Sometimes they pricked him with knives, sometimes they struck him with withes or touched lighted cigarettes to his flesh. It was all done with an air of rowdy abandon but with considered care, for it was not their purpose to wound him fatally until they were ready. They meant to save him alive for this very moment.

The man Harker sensed that the moment had come and must not be delayed. The Negro would soon be safe. Already his head had fallen forward and to one side. A light-colored bloody foam breathed out of the damaged lungs clung to the slack lips. Harker tried the flesh with the point of the knife. The Negro's head jerked a little.

Before raising his right hand with the knife in it, the dark man turned and looked briefly at the mob. It stood waiting without movement except that marking the rhythm of its quickened breath. It knew without it having been announced what the man Harker was going to do. It felt it in its own middle. Poised in its collective body it waited with yearning expectancy, like a woman's for the hard, harsh thrust of love, for the knife to lift and descend and cut clean away the stony pestle which pounds in its acknowledged mortar the unthinkable bread.

The man Harker's lifted hand trembled. He waited an instant to still the trembling. It must be clean and complete. He heard the suck of indrawn breath in the mob behind him as he reached forward. Suddenly the knife flashed and descended and he cast away what his left hand had clutched as the blood spurted behind the knife.

At that the Negro's heart fluttered and stopped. Nothing had heard or heeded his anguished prayer, unvoiced as he stumbled from Miss Ella's house, that his life would be spared because it was his and he possessed it and would have no other. With his heart's stoppage whatever meager dreams had animated his spirit were snuffed utterly. At the exact instant of his death he ceased to be that singular thing which was a man and which henceforth forever neither dominations nor powers could redeem or restore.

It was finished.

Eastward the darkness gathered upon the face of the waters, and at that place the earth would lie darkened for a span, but by due night.

The man Harker cut the rope that supported the body of the Negro and left it swinging by the neck before he turned again to the mob. The blood on his hands was already sticky. He flexed his hands, hearing the tearing, tacky sound they made with a deep revulsion. When he turned his eyes from his own hands and looked at the men about him, as in that optical illusion where what has been stared at intently or for a long time is repeated wherever one looks, it seemed to him that the hands of all the crowd were red with blood.

The mob dispersed abruptly, suddenly, with common consent. The men hurried out of the hills toward the town of Tilden. When they had gone from the place they felt better about it and began to look at each other as men will to share mutual understanding or relief. But then each man dropped his eyes, for it was a witness each saw when he looked into the face of his fellow.

# XXIX

THE DARK boy Farley and his feigned page Jonathan clung to each other while the sound of the men disappearing down the ridge grew less and ceased. After a while it was not from fear they clung under cover of the underbrush which had screened them from discovery by the men.

When they parted Jonathan put his hand to himself and touched the wetness against his flesh. The image of the Reverend Mr. Carhorn and the memory of his text had vanished from his mind. The boy Farley lay a moment with closed eyes treasuring the knowledge his hands had of the blond boy. Then he sat up and they looked at each other. Lot's visitants did not appear. Neither did anything prophesy of the sacrificial wife, a savor of salt wasted on the sterile plain.

Soon they left their hiding place in the shadow of the natural leaf on Hester's Ridge and followed after the men.

# XXX

AFTER HE encountered Mr. Darlington, the father of the boy Farley returned to the library, and for a while he sat brooding there. Then of a sudden he left the library and hurried down the street to Clarey's garage. It had come to him in a flash how he could save the life of the Negro Dandelion, and he walked with the brisk and determined stride of a man who knows what he is about.

"I want to rent a car for the day," he said to the attendant at Clarey's, "I may be going out of town."

"Sure," the attendant said. He moved among the few cars parked on the floor of the garage with legarthic unhaste, looking at them as if he expected to find himself betrayed by a tire gone flat or a collapsed wheel. "You can have this one if you like," he said, and he indicated a battered model.

The father of the boy Farley looked at the car in complete ignorance. Had it been a chariot of Samothrace he should have known its working parts but he knew nothing of automobiles except how to drive one provided it was in good mechanical condition and behaved in the expected manner when the gears were shifted from one ratio to another. "This doesn't look like it would run very fast," he said.

"Ain't nothing to the way they look," the attendant said. "It's a good little car. Run as fast as you want it to." He patted the car's fender as he might a horse's flank, looking at the professor of History at Tilden High as if he were somehow obligated to put his observation to the proof.

Farley's father made an impatient gesture and looked for a car of a newer model.

"Got a new one over there," the attendant said. "Going out of town, you say?"

"Yes," said the father of the boy Farley.

"Rented cars to lots of people today. All said they was going out of town."

"I'll take the new car," Farley's father said, making his words an evasion and a refusal to satisfy the desire of the attendant to know where he was going.

"Regular field day for us," the attendant said. "Sure a lot of people going out of town."

"This one will do," Farley's father said, indicating the new car. He held out his hand for the keys.

He got under the wheel and pushed impatiently at the starter button. The motor roared to life and he let out the clutch too quickly and the car bucked backwards until he brought it to a rocking halt by applying the brakes. The attendant looked at him dubiously, advancing on him again as the professor of History sat still a moment synchronizing in his thoughts the actions he must make to get a smooth start. The professor expected the attendant to comment on the rustiness of his driving. Instead he pursued the set of his single-minded thought.

"Any to-do around you know of?" the attendant shouted above the sound of the motor.

"None that I know of," Farley's father said. It struck him as incredible that the attendant should not know why his rentals had skyrocketed.

"Lots of people going *somewhere,*" the attendant shouted as Farley's father backed roaring from the garage. The vexed stare of the attendant followed him to the street.

When he was on the street he drove swiftly through the empty town. All he had to do was to load the Negro Dandelion in the automobile and carry him to some town or to the house of some other colored people he would find and leave him in safety until the furor in Tilden blew itself out.

It was all very simple. He did not know why he had not thought of it at first. Perhaps it was because he had never owned an automobile. He could not afford a car on his salary as a professor of History at Tilden High. The struggle to maintain himself and his family decently on his teacher's pittance was beginning to wear on him. He had never quite understood how one was to believe in the importance of one's work while wearing frayed collars. Though he was devoted to history, he was beginning to wonder if he shouldn't have chosen some other profession, the plumbing profession perhaps. His mind assembled its sets of comparative figures, and he snorted all of a sudden at the pretension to learning of that society which spends more on the disposal of its excrement than on the cultivation of the mind.

By now he had reached Center Street. He braked the car too suddenly and it swerved to the side. He took the turn too short and scraped the curb. In a few moments he turned from Center Street onto the street of no name.

When he pulled up before Dandelion's rickety shack he saw at once that he was too late, and as he traced the sign of struggle and foray about the chicken coop and leading from the house and to the street's edge, because he had delayed with them he cursed Mr. Darlington and the Reverend Mr. Carhorn with all the sulphur of his breath.

He called Dandelion's name. He went hopelessly beyond the coop to the house and stood in the breached door and called, speaking the name of Dandelion to the mean interior that had housed him in a slow, hushed voice, as if afraid his speech might raise from the stench of the cabin an outraged ghost.

Because he wished it not to be now but earlier, with time still to effect his plan, the scene and the day and the atmosphere of his thoughts began to take on an aura of unreality, as in the future of a dream. Then a reversal was accomplished with the cinematic effect of a card bearing inscriptions on both sides flicked over in a motion too swift for the eye, and the day's events were given to the keep of his great concern: History.

As though it were an obligation he was thinking: This is now, and this is the township of Tilden. He thought this as he walked to the rented car swift with the power of many horses and loud with thunder in its combustion chambers.

The car might as well have been a chariot, and the time B.C., and the place the kingdom of Thebes.

# XXXI

THE HUNTER Nimrod Anse, trailed by his dogs, was going into the hills and it seemed that night followed him, a flock of shadows amongst the mouthing hounds. The path he took led up the face of a peak called Craggy Bald. The base of the peak had been cleared and tilled and when he was a little way up the whole town could see him as he mounted with long tireless strides, leaning into the mountain as if probing with his eyes for the spoor of that quarry which he never found. The line demarking light and shadow was clearly defined behind him. It lifted as the sun sank lower and the hunter climbed on into the hills stalked by the shadow of night.

Below in the darkening town people sat before their doors as usual through the calm, long twilight. By four o'clock in the afternoon life in the town had resumed. Men left their places of business at the accustomed hour and went home, walking, if they walked, filled with a sense of the goodness of life to be going home to rest in the cool at the close of the summer day. If anything unusual marked the behavior of the men as they sat with their families after supper it was an abstracted restlessness. They paid little attention to what was said to them and they could not sit still for long at a time. Every once in a while a man would rise and stare toward the hills to the west of the town, and then sit down again. No one spoke of the day's event except for a loud-mouthed braggart here and there who in all likelihood had not been in at the kill. These when they spoke were shushed with a foul word or a dark look. By good dark several men of Tilden who were not notably inclined toward drink lay already in drunken stupor on porch floors or fully dressed across beds, or by the street wherever drunkenness overtook them.

Somewhere a dog howled and from the surrounding countryside a chorus answered him.

As night came the woman Angelicia was in her garden. She walked surrounded by the expectant cats. Now and then she raised her voice and called the name of her niece into the still evening air.

The woman Angelicia understood the nature of shadows and could distinguish between those elongated from the westward hills and that which was of a dangling figure hanging from a black oak limb. Of neither had she any fear.

"Rhoda!" the woman called into the garden, her voice colored with the concern her mind had for the Negro Dandelion. As she thought of him her chief regret was that at the time of his request she had refused him the beggarly sum of a quarter to meet she knew not what modest need. For a moment she was weighted with that emotion a parent might feel remembering refusal of a toy to a child who no more would play. Yet, she comforted herself, she had not really refused him. She had only forgotten his request in her concern for the cat which had disappeared.

"Tawm!" Angelicia called.

Really! thought the woman. While amending the name of the cat to that of her niece whom she sought she lifted her eyes and looked toward the face of Craggy Bald and saw the hunter climbing there. His figure was still touched by the sun, but while she looked he paused and turned and looked back toward the town. For a long moment he looked, as a man might in taking farewell. When he went forward again he hurried, for the receding daylight which had followed him at first outdistanced him in his pause and left him in pursuit.

In the place where the woman was the shadows deepened. It was part of her wisdom, or, she sometimes thought, only indicative of her age, that she knew if the hunter reached the summit of his mountain before nightfall the light would elude him there. He could pursue it no farther.

As for the Negro Dandelion, the sin of commission which the town of Tilden had that day committed against him troubled her, but she had reached a plateau in living where things were more of an equity. Neither good nor evil were of much stature as measured against her remaining years, so, for her, the Negro's shadow was a short one. Though it was without threat of degradation, circumstance foretold for her an end as barren as that of the Negro Dandelion. She saw how it was to come, as she did, without issue to the end of life. She saw how that which was seeded in indefinable time past, though through others it might prosper for countless generations yet, in herself reached extinction. If the figure be a tree, she thought, she was the fruitless branch. Or if fruit, once she was cast nothing could engraft part or parcel of herself anew to the temporal bough.

"Rhoda!" Angelicia called again, bearing heavily within her the thought of her fruitlessness. By now she was near the summer house, and suddenly her niece appeared before her as if she had materialized from the twilight air.

"My dear!" the woman Angelicia said, "where have you been?"

"I was asleep," Rhoda said, her voice contrite. She did not mean to tell her aunt how she had been hiding into her grace again since before the boy Farley discovered her behind the summerhouse.

"But where *were* you?" Aunt Angelicia said.

"Where Tawm . . ." Rhoda began but the voice of her aunt broke in upon her speech.

"We will forget Tawm, shan't we?" she said firmly.

"But it wasn't Tawm. It wasn't the cat," Rhoda said, looking into the eyes of Aunt Angelicia. She did not know how to explain it.

"I know what it was, Child," Angelicia said, remembering the girl and the two boys on the day which was yesterday. She herself hardly knew how she knew, only that there were always present like molds to be filled, or faint like memories, impressions in crushed grass, in straw, in darkness, of supine flesh locked in the thresh of discovery, locked in the aggression of love.

The eyes of the old woman had lost the agate hardness they had that morning when she looked at her niece now. There was still no weakness in them, but resignation and acceptance of reality. She knew that the dream of the figure in the tulle gown which she had recaptured might yet be somehow terminated or qualified, but she felt like a divination that though she was old she might still see the fulfillment of her dream.

"Oh, my dear!" the woman Angelicia said to her niece in affectionate warmth. She placed her old arm about the young shoulders and together they walked slowly to the house, through the darkening garden where the cannas glowed dull red in the dusk, like banked fires.

Not far away from Angelicia's the cleaning woman stood in the door of Miss Ella's house nursing an elbow in each hand while she stared into the street. For a long while no one came from the direction in which the heart of the town lay, and she felt isolated, alone, except when the high, light voice of Miss Ella speaking to unseen presences broke the silence in the house.

After a while a solitary man came up from the town and she accosted him. When she spoke the man turned his face aside as if he had not heard her and made as to pass on. She pressed after him with her voice, asking about the Negro's death, wanting details in her proprietary interest in the event.

The man said nothing. He stood hesitant where he had halted, compelled by courtesy and by something in the woman's voice that touched him where no hand might. He stood with his eyes turned aside. He had been that day in the hills to the west of the town.

The cleaning woman thought the man simple or drunk.

"She wasn't, you know," she thrust finally at the man, into his silence, and he lifted his eyes suddenly, startled, incredulous. She laughed at his discomfiture, and as he went on up the street stood remembering Mary Brophy saying: *But we must never mention it. Think how the poor men would feel!*

Before the man was fully out of sight it grew too dark to see him. Miss Ella's petulant voice came from within and the cleaning woman turned into the house again. She made a comforting clucking sound as she gave Miss Ella a drink of water; then she took a cloth and dipped it and wiped the other's forehead.

Miss Ella had a fever. The doctor Mary Brophy had called discovered this at the same time he discovered that she had not been violated.

But we must never mention it! the cleaning woman said to herself in a mimic of Mary Brophy's voice, perverting the meaning of the words to comment on her own reluctant virginity.

She knew the fact of the Negro's innocence would not keep. Besides herself Mary Brophy and the doctor knew of it. Something in her stilled as she remembered the solitary man and his lifted, startled eyes. Perhaps now, even, he imparted his doubts, his dread of the truth to another and the shadow of the victim lengthened in the light of its innocence.

Miss Ella began to speak again to some unseen presence. All at once the cleaning woman envied Miss Ella the possession of her phantoms. She began to rock in the chair by Miss Ella's bed, and after a while in the unlighted darkness of full night she drowsed and dreamed. In her dream she saw a lame figure with averted eyes shuffling slowly up the street of no name.

Across town at first dark the half-caste Cracker emerged gingerly from a shed at the sawmill near Clifton Mills where he had been in hiding since afternoon. When the mob on its way from the mill passed him that afternoon someone took a pot shot at him with a revolver, and the unpausing mob laughed at his antic leap which spilled the sack full of shavings he was carrying for the Reverend Mr. Carhorn's chicken house and carried him half the distance back to the planing shed. The man had purposely fired wide. It was not the bastard's blood they were after, but Cracker hid himself in terror to await darkness.

It had been his plan to slip out of town when night came, but the darkness found him with as great a fear of venture as he had earlier had of the men. He meant now to return to the shed-room of the pastor's house where he slept. The memory of the stately strength of the Reverend Mr. Carhorn reassured him. He would soon be near that presence. Yet when he was halfway to the preacher's house and heard voices on the street he dodged into the shadow of a building and stood splayed against the wall as if affixed by darts until the unseen passers were gone.

Twice he had to hide before reaching the preacher's house, but once within sight of it he met a stroller on the street openly and the man greeted him with a half-contemptuous hail and nod. The ingenuous Cracker followed the man with his eyes, feeling himself at once restored to his place as before.

He thought then of the Negro Dandelion and of their encounter of the morning. "You ain't neither, you ain't nothin'," the Negro Dandelion had said, and it was true. His white blood had not made him white, but now that the Negro Dandelion had been subtracted from the town's two digits of dark flesh he felt himself something sole.

In a gesture he had, he locked his fingers and knocked the heels of his hands together in time to some inner rhythm. He began to strut.

I'm *somethun!* he said to himself.

Elsewhere a figure stumbled its way through darkness toward the bench of earth on Hester's Ridge where since afternoon the body of Dandelion had swung from the black oak limb. While the day decreased the body of the slain man had swung under the limb, turning this way or that to suit the wind. It was all the same to it.

Once a bird made an exploratory flight over the body and finding nothing to fear came and perched on the shoulder. It pecked speculatively at the flesh, then cleaned and whetted its bill and sang.

The bird flew away and the body was alone again.

The professor of History at Tilden High could tell he was near what he sought by the odor that rode on the wind. It was not of putrescence exactly, but a sweetish sickening stench that is sometimes about slaughtering pens.

When he had found it, after much fumbling and groping in the double darkness beneath the leaves by the ineffectual pencil of the flashlight beam, the professor of History at Tilden High took the body of the Negro Dandelion; and he buried it among the valiant of the kingdom of Thebes.

About this same time, among the cleanly odors of his life the farmer Abraham sat down to supper. The smell of the fresh-baked bread, the smell of Sarah's garments, freshly laundered and ironed, and the rich odor of strength from his sons' scrubbed hands all mingled in the long room that was the kitchen and the family dining room. The dying fire from the stove on which supper had been cooked added to the heat gathered from the August day and retained under the low shedded roof, but a breeze that usually blew at that altitude was springing up and its intermittent fan breathed through the kitchen door, an open oblong near the top of which the first star of evening glowed.

Sarah sat at the opposite end of the table from Abraham and on either side the faces of his sons were lighted before him in sober regard. As the shadow of the Negro touched the woman Angelicia but a little, it touched the family of Abraham not at all. Before threat he, a simple man, had found the strength to believe the truth, and something was added to the heritage of Abraham's sons, and his sons' sons and daughters still unborn, that would bestead them in dark hours in the future that was theirs.

"Do you know?" Abraham was saying. He spoke to his wife Sarah though for his sons to hear also, watching her patient gray eyes that somehow always told him what she was thinking even when she did not speak.

"Well," Abraham went on, "I saw a hawk."

"A hawk, Abraham?"

"Yes." He saw that Sarah and his sons waited, his wife's present patience merely a continuation of that which she had always shown. He tried. "Yes. They threatened me, too, but of course I was not afraid of them."

"No," Sarah said, as if she meant: Indeed not.

"And the Negro wasn't afraid of them either then. They carried him into the hills after that and I didn't see them anymore. But just before, I saw the hawk."

"Do you think it was . . ." Sarah began, and then she waited, but Abraham said nothing immediately. "Was it, do you think . . . ?" She was trying to say it for him without taking it away from him.

"Well, yes," he said. Then he said, his face suffused with color and the arteries of his neck corded and nearly choking him, "Well, I can say what I believe. I saw the hawk and it was not a hawk."

He looked at Sarah's pale, patient face and wanted to say something more, but nothing came. He could not shape the words. In the silence that followed his speech the family fell to eating with heartiness. He looked at their faces and he knew then that beyond the death of them all the hawk would lift. Except the sun the hawk, Abraham thought as he poised his fork above his plate, and forever the hawk; the hawk and the sun.

**THE END**